WHY ISN'T SCH[illegible]

MORE LIKE SHOPPING?

Pete Edwards

filmpro

WHY ISN'T SCHOOL MORE LIKE SHOPPING?

ISBN 978-1-914458-40-8

First published September 2024 by
filmpro through P2D Books Ltd

cover collage and design: Zeynep Dağlı

Printed and bound in Great Britain by
www.p2dbooks.co.uk
Westoning, Bedfordshire

WHY ISN'T SCHOOL MORE LIKE SHOPPING?

CHAPTER 1

Downstairs was yet another Saturday night party at home with my Mum and Dad's family and their friends from the local pub. My dad would always bring his friends home after a big drinking session. My mum would be at home entertaining the wives, having a drink and a good natter, also making sandwiches for everybody for when the men came back from the pub.

That was when the noise would begin, with music, singing and dancing. Everyone would gather in our large, brightly decorated living room, singing along to Vince Hill's *Love Letters in the Sand*. I have a distant memory of them singing that song, the sound echoing around my dimly lit bedroom waking me from a wonderful sleep. My arm reached out and my tiny fingers grabbed hold of one of the bars of the white cot like shit sticking to a blanket. Letting go was not an option. I started to scream sodding blue murder. My Aunty Helen, Mum's only sister, came into my room. She was wearing a red silk dress and black high-heeled shoes.

Half-pissed on Scotch, she prised my tightly closed fingers off the bar of my cot. Then she picked me up to comfort me and I stopped crying and fell back to sleep. Not only because my aunty was hugging me, but probably as the smell of scotch helped to knock me out.

After a short stint behind cot bars, Mum and Dad bought me my first single bed. It had a brown wooden headboard decorated with Winnie the Pooh stickers. Oh how I loved my Winnie and Christopher Robin.

Early life was fantastic. I was one of three children. Mum had Sean first, April second, and last but not least, me. As the youngest child, I was spoiled with both love and attention.

We had wonderful times in our four-bedroom, semi-detached house. My mum was short and plump with white curly hair. She was a very kind and loving lady. She had been born in Dublin and had emigrated to London when she was eighteen. My mum would do absolutely anything for anyone. Being brought up as a Catholic and attending a school that had been run by nuns, my mum was very strict regarding religion and going to church every Sunday.

Mum worked as a cleaner before I was born, and some years after I arrived, took another job as a school cook. On top of her paid employment she also took care of all the family.

Unlike Mum, Dad was very tall and thin, with wispy, dark brown hair. He had been born in Plymouth and was one of nine children. However, like my mum, I remember he was always happy, always laughing, and just loved life.

Dad worked as a carpenter for the whole of his adult life and his yard was just next door to our house. I loved the smell of the sawdust when Dad came in the back door from work. I may have loved that smell but Mum hated it, because the wood chippings he bought in with him made a mess of our home, which drove my mother crazy. Luckily she had a solution.

She bought us a budgie named Joey. Every day when Dad got back from work, he would now open the door of the budgie's cage and the bird would fly around the kitchen a few times before settling on Dad's head. Dad would sit and read his paper while the bird picked the sawdust out of his hair.

A couple of years after my mum and dad got married, Dad decided to change his faith to match my mother's, converting from Protestant to Catholic. As my mum insisted on the whole family going to church every Sunday, I think my dad just thought, 'If you can't beat them, join them.'

However, this caused a lot of animosity and tension with Dad's family, which was very difficult for him and us for some time.

While life was great most of the time, when we argued as a family the Battle of Britain had nothing on us.

For an unknown reason I was a bloody nightmare as a baby, which no doubt aggravated my parents' arguments. I would never stop crying, and giving me the bottle or a dummy was near impossible because it appeared as if I was unable to suck.

My elegant maternal grandmother also lived with us. Her husband had sadly passed away before I was born so I never got to meet my grandad, although she told me many stories about his life.

She was a tremendous help for Mum when I came into the world. She would spend hours holding me in her arms, rocking me backward and forward in her rocking chair trying to get me to sleep. But it hardly ever worked.

Grandma was a tiny lady who had lovely silver-grey hair that was always pinned up. She wore a pinafore every day of her life. Well, as far as I can remember she did! She was tough and strict with us at times but she had a lot of love for us too.

My grandma spent bloody days and weeks trying to give me the bottle but it was just impossible. One day Mum and Grandma had a

Eureka moment. It was the day they found and bought me a baby cup and at last I was able to have a proper drink. Boy, was I thirsty! I remember another brilliant day when Grandma made me a cup of coffee and I have never looked back. I have to say I'm completely addicted to the stuff. So thank you very much, Grandma!

The months passed and my mum and dad began to worry about me more and more every day. One Saturday lunchtime Dad said to Mum whilst eating a ham sandwich, "I think it's time to go back to the doctors with Adam, Rose."

"Terry," my Mum replied, "I understand what you're saying but I'm just sick and tired of hearing doctors and specialists saying there is nothing wrong with Adam. He's just a very late developer."

As Mum took a sip of tea and picked up her sandwich, she added, "We have two other children darling, so we should know by now if there is a problem with one of them."

Dad said, "Love, I do understand how you feel," and he put his arms around Mum's shoulders as she started to cry.

"Darling, we have to find out why he is still not able to sit, crawl, or hold his head up at eighteen months without support," he added.

Mum said, "I'll try to get an appointment at the doctor's next week."

"I think that's a good idea, love, because we have to get to the bottom of this for all our sakes."

On the next Monday morning my mum said, "April, can you watch Adam for Mummy please? I'll lay him on the rug in the living room. Give him his toys and play with him please, darling, just while Mummy makes some telephone calls."

April replied, "I'll get his big spinning top, that's one of his favourites."

As April began to spin the brightly coloured top, my arms began to move with excitement, my eyes lit up, and I broke into a lovely, big smile.

"Look Mummy. Adam is reaching for it," April shouted very happily.

"Yes I know, my love, it's wonderful," said Mum, looking down at me whilst rubbing gently on April's head and saying, "You are a good girl for looking after Adam for Mummy," before walking out of the room, drying her eyes.

April called after her, "Can I have some sweeties, Mummy?"

"Alright. I'll bring some when I am off the phone," agreed Mum.

After speaking to the doctors and the specialists came weeks of testing before they called my parents to the hospital with news of the outcome.

Mum and Dad were called into Dr Easton's office. It was a large room with white walls and a couch on the left-hand side. The doctor sat down behind his desk, and looking at them without any outward expression said, "Your son is disabled with cerebral palsy. He will never walk and you shouldn't expect him to live past eight years old. So my advice to you is to put him away in a children's home."

Mum and Dad were distraught but very quickly made their decision to keep me. Thank God Mum and Dad came to the right decision and I stayed with my family. Life carried on, playing with April and Sean and muddling along, getting my very first little wheelchair which gave me my first small taste of independence.

Unfortunately that wasn't quite the end of my problems, because at the age of two I had my first epileptic fit, which was very frightening for me and my parents. I had to go for lots more tests and had to put on a lovely brown rubber cap for a test called an electroencephalogram (E.E.G.) and boy, did I hate that bloody test.

The doctor, Doctor Palmer, was a very straight-laced woman. She was quite tall with black curly hair and green piercing eyes. When I was having the test, I used to scream blue murder, and Dad had to hold me whilst the doctor put plugs on my head with glue. I am sure Dad would have liked some glue for my mouth to stop me screaming.

That was the first of many screaming sessions with this specialist. I am sure she had a stack of earplugs for my appointments. Boy, she was a grumpy cow!

After my first E.E.G. Mum and Dad brought me home from the hospital and I was sitting on Dad's lap with my white ankle boots on. My grandma gave me my Christmas present early, just because they all thought I was very ill and was going to die.

It was a fantastic, bright blue minicar. How I loved my Mini. At home we had a lovely, large garden that Dad was very proud of. It had a big square of concrete that was surrounded with flower beds which contained Dad's favourites, which were geraniums. Unfortunately, they smelled of cat's pee if you got too close to them. There were many beautiful flowering shrubs around the edge.

I used to love riding my Mini around while Sean and April were on their scooters. My dad also had a large shed in the garden where he would do most of his woodwork. At times he would make us toys. I can think back to when Dad made us a large green train engine with a black funnel that Sean or April could push me along in, in the garden.

The first part of my life was quite difficult for me, especially because I never liked going to nursery from the age of two.

Land Field Grove School was where I began having a bloody life of physiotherapy! As well as being my nursery, Land Field Grove was also my infant and primary school. When I started there my mum had to take me in a mini cab. I used to scream and kick the hell out of her on the way.

When we arrived, Mrs. Widgery, my nursery teacher, who was a very tall lady with a young soft face and always wore dark clothes, would say to Mum, who was sweating with exhaustion as she took me, "Good morning, Mrs. King, and hello, Adam. Shall we go to the nursery and let Mummy go to have a cup of tea?"

"Bye bye, Adam. I love you. Have a good day," Mum said, kissing me.

Mrs. Widgery, my nursery school teacher, always laid me on a small, soft, wool rug and left me to have a roll around and have a stretch.

After our freedom of rolling around and playing, we had to begin bloody physiotherapy. A physio would support the same child each day.

My physio was called Mrs. Britten. She had golden-brown curly hair and a wonderful smile. She was great most of the time. Every day she wore dark blue trousers and a white smock top with dark blue edging around the collar.

"Good morning, Adam. How are you today?" Mrs. Britten would ask, kicking her black clogs off and sitting on the carpet with me. Then she would strip me down to my vest and pants.

In front of every rug there was a long mirror so that the children could look at themselves whilst doing their exercises.

Most days Mrs. Britten said, "Can you look at yourself in the mirror for me, Adam?"

I tried to lift my very wobbly head up to look at myself. Another exercise I remember was being hung upside down by my ankles and yes, I know it was to help straighten my body, but it scared the bloody life out of me back then!

At this point most children had to do the same, and the classroom was full of commotion, with children screaming and crying out of fear.

Looking back at that time, I think it was very disconcerting and somewhat sinister!

Also, being sat on a wooden stool and being told by the physio: "Don't let me push you off, don't let me push you off, don't let me push you off!" whilst pushing me gently on the arm was a very strange thing to do and say to a disabled child that had no sodding balance.

I began nursery school at about the age of two because of my condition. My parents had to start reporting back to doctors and specialists regarding my intelligence and how much I would be able to do for myself. Obviously, they were discovering more as time went on and as I got older.

During my time at nursery school there are some moments I can remember quite vividly.

When I began infant school I was thin and very lanky and had brown hair. Mrs. Ryan was my first teacher. She was a short lady, with black hair that was tied in a ponytail almost every day.

I had three best friends called Gordon, Clinton and Nick. We were inseparable.

Gordon had cerebral palsy and he walked with sticks. He had black hair and green eyes. He was short for his age and just a little bit tubby. He was forever getting himself into trouble.

Clinton was a quiet lad. His disability was spina bifida and he was in a wheelchair. He was very skinny with blue eyes and he also had black hair. Nick's disability was cerebral palsy. He was in a wheelchair, and like me, he pushed himself around school with his feet. He spoke with a mild speech impediment. Nick had ginger hair and green eyes and his favourite game just like the other two boys was playing *Tag*.

In the mornings Mrs. Ryan always began by asking all the children to sit together on the floor with our physios to support us sitting up. We would sing the good morning song, which went like this: "Good morning, Adam and how are you? Good morning, Adam. How do you do?"

After that Miss would ask each of us to pass a coloured brick to one another and hold on to it whilst we said what colour it was, which was harder than you would think when you find it very hard to grip anything and have a speech impediment.

In the afternoons it was time for a pet hate of my life: speech therapy.

Mrs. Turner, our speech therapist, was a tall Black lady with great frizzy hair. She also had a great sense of humour. Speech therapy was a very difficult thing for me and some of the other children because our speech was never going to be very clear anyway. Mrs. Turner would also put horrible substances on our lips, which were all disgusting. Then we would have to try and lick the stuff off with our tongues, yucky!! Physiotherapy and speech therapy were always in my life, which was a bit of a bugger!

I can also remember playing with toy bricks and plasticine. Water and sand play was also great fun as a young child and getting covered in paint was really satisfying. I recall bringing home my very first painting. It was blue and red spots. My mum put it on the kitchen wall, which made her (and me) very proud. It was my one and only Van Gogh moment!

"You're a street angel and a house devil!" Those were the words my mum said to me many a time in her lovely Irish accent. I was a ticking time bomb, light the touch paper and 1, 2, 3, bang! I was off. Furniture was kicked, cupboards were rammed, and Grandma gets another bruise on her leg.

Mum shouted, "How many times, Grandma! Please don't get in the way when he is in this mood, then you won't get hurt."

All just because I wanted to play a game with Sean and April before tea, but Dad had said, "Wait until after tea to play your game, Son."

During my tantrum, Dad would suddenly pick me up out of my wheelchair whilst I was screaming, kicking, and punching. He would take me to the bedroom, put me on the bed, go out, and shut the door. Then I would just cry and shout. After I had calmed down, Mum would come in and talk to me.

I would say, "Sorry, Mum. I will never do that again," and I honestly meant it - until the next time!

Moving up the years in infant school, I began to enjoy it a bit more, not that I ever really enjoyed school.

But reading *Peter and Jane* books, playing footy at playtime with my mates (although I never understood why I always had to go in goal!!) and also having water fights when we got a chance, were brilliant. However, getting in trouble by the headmistress was shit.

Miss Manton, the headmistress, was a short lady with grey hair. She wore blue-rimmed glasses that hung on a chain around her neck. She was very strict and walked with a limp.

One bright Tuesday morning Mum and Dad were asked to come up to the school to see her.

'Bloody hell, I'm in trouble,' I thought. 'Bang goes my new Osmonds album. That's a shit.' I was so looking forward to having it. I was in Mr. Howard's class. He was a stocky man, quite tall, and he had a black moustache which he would twiddle when teaching us.

Well, I say teaching, because every day at 11 am we would have to watch a *Who, What, Where and Why* program. Which was about work in factories, supermarkets, on a building site or a farm. The list goes on and on.

But on that very particular Tuesday morning I didn't care how bread was bloody made! No, my mind was on what Miss Manton was talking to my parents about. It could have been about how hard I'm working in school, or about my talking in lessons, but they are so boring and chatting to my friends like Nick is much more fun. Or it could have been how I wheeled down the corridor knocking children over, but then again, it's not my fault if they get in the bloody way! Just then the door of the classroom opened and Miss Manton asked Mr. Howard if I could go to her office now please.

Clinton whispered, "Don't worry, mate. The worst you'll get is the cane or lines."

"Shut it, Clinton," I hissed back.

Then Mr. Howard really shouted at me, "Stop talking and go with Miss Manton now, Adam!"

"Yes, Sir. Sorry, Sir."

On the way down the corridor to her office, Miss Manton said, "Are you alright, Adam?"

"Yes, thank you, Miss," I responded, but what I really wanted to say was, "No, I'm petrified, Miss, because my parents are in your office, and I might be on my way there to get told off, and I have never been called to the head's office." Oh, bloody hell!!

"Hello, Son," Dad said.

"Hello, Mum. Hello, Dad," I said, trying to read their faces as my dad said his favourite phrase to me: "Stop dribbling and sit up straight, Adam, for God's sake," as he wiped my chin with his hanky.

"Yes, Dad."

Miss Manton walked around and sat behind her desk.

Then she said, "Adam, your mum, dad and I have been talking, and I have also spoken to Mr. Howard. We feel that a new school would be a good move for you."

I looked at Mum very worriedly as she said, "I agree that a new school is right for you, Adam."

Then Dad added, "It will benefit you a lot too."

I felt my lower lip quiver.

"No, I like it here. I will miss my friends. Why do I have to go to a new school?"

My mum took my hand.

"Adam, of course you'll still be able to see your friends. Clinton, Nick and Gordon can come to tea sometimes. Also you're going to make new friends as well."

Dad then said, looking at me, "Listen, Son, your mum and I have been talking to Miss Manton over the past few weeks, and Miss Manton feels, and your mum and I agree with her, that Land Field Grove School has offered all it can to you and a new school would benefit you now."

Miss Manton then added, "Bright Side is a very good school, Adam. So why don't you just go to have a look at it with Mum and Dad next week? You might like it?"

"I don't know, Miss," I replied, starting to cry, hoping that this would go away, because I was very happy where I was.

Then Mum looked at Dad and said, "I'm sorry, Terry, but we have to be honest with the boy."

"Would you like me to explain to him what we have been talking about?" said Miss Manton.

'I wish someone would bloody hurry up and explain to me what's going on,' I thought.

"Adam, you're going to have to be a big boy for me. Can you do that?"

"Yes, Miss," I responded, frightened about what she was going to say.

"Right, Adam. Bright Side is a fantastic school for children with disabilities. However, it's a boarding school. Do you know what that is?"

I went quiet, as I had heard of a school like that before. One of Clinton's friends had to go to one and they told him it was horrible.

Dad said to me, "Come on, Adam, answer Miss Manton please."

Getting very distressed, I shouted out: "Yes, yes, I do know what a boarding school is, Miss."

Dad finally said to me, "Adam, we are very proud of you Son, and Mum and I want the best for you. So next Wednesday morning we have an appointment to go and see Bright Side School to see if they will offer you a place, and I'm sure they will. You are going to have to board from Monday to Friday."

"No, Mum, please. I don't want to go away to school. I love being here and I'll miss everybody. Please don't make me go. Have I been naughty or bad? I'm sorry if I have."

I began to cry. Dad was getting a bit upset with me.

"Stop the tears now. You haven't been naughty, that's got nothing to do with this."

With that, Miss Manton said, "Adam, I know you're worried and scared, that's understandable. Why don't you talk it over with Mum and Dad and we can all discuss it further in a couple of weeks?"

Mum answered, "I think that's a good idea, Miss Manton, and thank you very much for meeting with us today, and we'll let you know how we get on at the new school next Wednesday."

CHAPTER 2

Being brought up a very strict Catholic, I was expected to follow in the footsteps of Sean and April regarding our religion.

It was just after my eighth birthday and Mum said, "Adam, love, you're going to have to make your first holy communion in June of this year. I have spoken to Father Nicholas regarding your catechism, and he said it might be better for you if he comes here for an hour on Saturday morning to teach you about the Bible. As he doesn't think it would be right for you to go to Sunday school."

"Mum, no, do I have to learn about the Bible?"

April, who was in the kitchen with Mum and me, just glared at me while choking on her cornflakes, knowing Mum was about to shout, "How dare you say that? You're going to do something very special in your Catholic faith, and more importantly Father Nicholas has offered to come to our home and teach you. Show some respect, Adam, please."

So for about nine Saturday mornings, right in the middle of *The Osmonds* and *The Brady Bunch*, which also happened to be mine and April's favourite programmes on a Saturday, Mum would come in the lounge with a plate of biscuits which had a lace doily underneath that she'd prepared for Father Nicholas to eat while he was teaching me.

"April, turn off the television now and go to your room and do your homework please?" Mum always said, about ten minutes before Father Nicholas arrived.

The first week I began my catechism lessons, I felt very nervous. The front doorbell rang and Dad answered the door, saying, "Good morning, Father. How are you today?"

"I'm fine, thank you, Mr. King. It's quite a warm day," Father Nicholas replied, entering the lounge and removing his grey coat.

As he carried on saying, "Hello, Adam, are you alright? It's nice to see you, and I'm looking forward to teaching you about the Bible," I just gave him a smile and a nod.

Father Nicholas, our parish priest, was a tall man with a large frame. His hands were big and eyebrows were bushy and Mum and Dad liked him a lot.

Then Mum came into the lounge and said, "It's very nice to see you, Father. Can I get you a cup of tea before you begin?"

"Yes, Mrs. King, that would be lovely. Thank you."

After Mum had brought Father Nicholas' tea in to him, and of course it was in a china cup and saucer (because you wouldn't dare offer the priest anything else!), shutting the lounge door, Mum said, "Just shout if you need us, Father. Mr. King and I are only in the kitchen."

"Yes, we will, won't we, Adam?"

I gave another nod as I didn't know how to talk to him. Father Nicholas said, "Let us begin with the Lord's Prayer, Adam. Bow your head now, please."

After we had prayed, Father Nicholas just spoke at me and he showed me pictures from the Bible. After we'd finished the first session, Father Nicholas opened the door of the lounge.

Walking up the hallway with Dad behind, Mum said, "Did it all go alright, Father?"

"Yes, it went okay, I think. Adam and I looked at some picture cards from the Bible and he responded well to them."

"That's good news, Father, isn't it?" Mum asked with a worried look.

Then Father Nicholas said, "Yes, yes, yes, of course it's good news, Mr. and Mrs. King. Now, I'll see you in church tomorrow. So, have you any plans for next week?"

As Dad answered, "Well, Father, next Wednesday we are going to look at a new school for Adam. Aren't we, Son?"

"Yes, Dad," I replied quietly.

Putting his coat on, Father Nicholas said, "Wow, Adam, a new school. Are you excited?"

Mum said quite harshly, "No Father, he's not, because it's a boarding school where he will have to stay from Monday until Friday and he hates the idea. But it's a very good school for children like Adam."

"Thank you for today, Adam, and we'll carry on next Saturday, and I will see you all at ten o'clock Mass tomorrow," Father Nicholas said as Mum saw him out.

Later on that Saturday, before Dad sat down to do the football pools and Mum began to peel the potatoes for dinner, I was playing with my cars and Tonka trucks in my bedroom. Also thinking about the week ahead and wondering what the school might be like. Suddenly April came in and said, "Dad wants to see you in the kitchen."

"What for? I'm playing, and next time, knock. Anyway what does Dad want?" I whined.

"I don't know what Dad wants. He just asked me to come and call you."

When I got out into the kitchen I began to cry and push myself back up the hallway saying, "No, Dad, please," as I saw a large, bright red bath towel spread out on the kitchen table with a white pillow on top. This meant only one bloody thing for me. Dad was going to cut my hair, which I absolutely despised as a boy.

"Listen to me, Son. I say this to you every time before cutting your hair. If you don't struggle or fight it will be better for you, me, and everybody else."

Unfortunately, that just fell on deaf ears. Then my dad and Sean picked me up to lay me down on the kitchen table while I was screaming and kicking. When I was having my hair cut, Sean was holding my legs down, April was doing the same with my arms, and Mum held my head still for Dad to cut my hair short, because that was the way they preferred it.

After everything was over and I had been put back in my wheelchair, Mum gave me a cuddle.

She said, brushing the loose hairs from my neck, "You look very smart, Son, and that will be nice for when we go to see your new school on Wednesday. Won't it, Adam, love?"

"Yes, Mum. Can I go and play now?"

"Of course you can," Mum replied with a smile.

'Do I really have to go through this? Please God get me out of the dreaded nightmare that is about to hit my life,' I thought on the Wednesday morning when Mum, Dad and I were going to visit Bright Side School (for Handicapped Children).

As my dad was driving there I felt extremely sad and nervous. I just wanted to scream, "STOP Dad, no, no, no, please take me home, it's too far away." However, I knew there was no use.

When we arrived and Dad pulled up in the school car park, the school seemed larger than Land Field Grove. In fact when Mum and Dad lifted me out of our cream Volkswagen van that was adapted for me and my wheelchair, the school seemed massive. Mum, with Dad pushing me, walked over and up a slope into the entrance of my new school. I felt horrified as I knew I wasn't going to like the outcome of today.

Mrs. Pointer greeted us, saying, "Good morning, Mr. and Mrs. King, and you must be Adam. I'm Mrs. Pointer, the school secretary." She was in her late forties and she was very short, with tight, curly brown hair that looked a little bit like the top of a microphone, and wore horn-rimmed glasses that hung on a chain around her neck.

She carried on, saying, "Welcome to Bright Side School. Mr. Eaton, the headmaster, will be with you in a couple of minutes. Can I get you anything before I go back to my office?"

"No thank you, Mrs. Pointer," Dad replied.

"Okay then, nice to have met you, and hope to see you soon, Adam."

As Mrs. Pointer walked away, Mum said, "She is a nice lady. Isn't she, Son?"

"Yes, Mum," I answered, looking around, trying to get a feel of the place with children and staff going past while thinking about how I can get out of coming here.

A couple of minutes later, I found myself in Mr. Eaton's office with my mum and dad. The office was a square room which was painted a light shade of blue. There was a window looking out over the school car park. Mr. Eaton, who was tall with grey hair and green eyes, sat behind his desk in a red leather chair, and Mum and Dad sat on two black chairs. I just looked around the room that smelled of very highly polished wood while Mum, Dad and Mr. Eaton spoke about what the school could offer me.

Then Mr. Eaton asked, "Would you like to come to Bright Side School, Adam?"

Like a stupid fool, I said very shyly, "Yes."

"Well, let's go and have a look around school and you can meet some of the children. Mr. and Mrs. King, you can meet with Sister Gray, the school nurse, and with Mr. Williams, who will be Adam's house father, and Mrs. Hanson, his teacher."

The school was very large, like I said. The classrooms were in a gigantic rectangle with a playground in the centre. The boarding unit was just behind the classrooms and down a corridor leading off the school sports hall. Everything was becoming too real for me by the minute as we were looking around the school.

Before leaving, I had to wait outside Mr. Eaton's office so my mum and dad could have a private talk with him.

"Well, it was very good to meet you, Adam," Mr. Eaton said, after they had come out of his office.

"Yes, Mr. Eaton, thank you so much for today. Either me or Mrs. King will be in touch with you soon," Dad said, shaking his hand.

On our way home, we had to stop for shopping and a present for me, to bribe and convince me about the new school. I thought going shopping was fantastic a lot of the time. Unfortunately, not with Mum and Dad, as I would have to wait outside the shops. Especially shops like M&S, Sainsbury's and Cullen's. Sometimes I was joined by a little boy with callipers on, holding a big wooden box with a hole in the top for money. However, he couldn't speak as he was a statue. There were times I felt like that.

I was waiting outside Sainsbury's with my little friend whilst Mum and Dad were in the shop. Now what I liked about Sainsbury's when I was a child was, it was just one long shop with different counters either side, like meat, fish, and vegetables, and other kinds of food that you always had to ask for. What made me feel better was that I was able to see Mum and Dad when they were walking from side to side of the shop, buying the weekly groceries and treats for me. However, at other shops where I couldn't see my mum or dad through the window I would be worried, particularly when they were a long time. I would be very scared and wondering if they had forgotten about me, which never actually happened.

Afterwards, when we got home and Mum was putting away the groceries whilst feeding me the chocolate buttons I had chosen, she asked, "Well, did you like Bright Side School, Son?"

"It was alright, but I didn't like the uniform, Mum," I replied.

"Mr. Eaton the headmaster was very nice, wasn't he, Son?" asked Dad, making a cup of tea for Mum and himself.

Mum answered him before I got a chance to reply, "Yes, Terry. I thought Mr. Eaton and the other staff we met were very pleasant."

Eating another chocolate button, I had a wonderful idea, thinking this might be a way of getting me out of going to bloody Bright Side.

So I said excitedly, "Mum, Mum, Dad."

"Yes, Adam?" Dad said, sitting down at the kitchen table with his cup of tea.

"I don't have to leave Land Field Grove School until I'm eleven years old, and that's three years away. Am I right, Dad?"

My dad made a large sigh and looked over to my mum, who was sitting at the other end of the table.

"Adam, we had this conversation last Tuesday and yes, I know Miss Morton said that we should go back to talk to her. But Son, me and your mum were very happy, and we think Bright Side is an excellent school with a lot to offer you. So we would like you to go there now, and we spoke to Mr. Eaton today, and luckily they have a place they can offer you starting next Monday."

Feeling very sad and annoyed, I took myself up the hallway and sat beside the coat stand which was by our front door. This was one of the places I would go if I couldn't get my own way.

Whilst sitting there, Sean came in from school and said, "Hi, Adam. Did you have a good day? And how was your visit to the new school?"

"Shut up you twit and go to hell," I shouted.

Mum called up the passage, "Don't worry, Sean, love. Your dad and I have just told him that he's starting the new school on Monday, so that's why your brother is in a bad mood. If he carries on like that, I'll put him to bed without any ruddy tea."

"Adam, can I say something, please?" Sean asked, as he sat on the stairs undoing the laces of his school shoes.

"If you must," I replied.

"You're not doing yourself any favours with Mum and Dad behaving like this."

"Oh aren't I, Sean? Well, you go away to a bloody boy's boarding school, see how you like it. I suppose it's because I'm disabled," I responded in anger.

Then Sean got very mad at me. "What is your damn problem, Adam? Mum, Dad, or any of us have never ever treated you differently because you're disabled, and we wouldn't. Anyway you bloody know damn well that going to Bright Side is not about your disability, but more about the best school for you, and you'll only be gone from Monday until Friday. Get a grip, for Christ's sake."

Sean was tall with a bit of a tummy on him. He had long light brown hair which reached his shoulders and blue eyes. Sport was very much his passion, either playing or watching it. He was like Dad in that sense. Sean could be great fun or a complete moody arse, and God, did he have an attitude issue.

Suddenly Mum opened the kitchen door and said, "Sean, Adam, tea is ready. Sean, can you shout up to April for me, please? She's upstairs doing her homework."

April, walking down the stairs said, "Adam, are you coming to have some tea?"

"No, I don't want any," I sulked.

Then I heard a kitchen chair scraping on the floor and Dad saying to Mum, "Just leave him, Rose. You can sort him out after you've eaten."

"No, Terry, I'm too angry to eat. I am going to put Adam to bed now. April, can you come and help me with Adam, please?" Mum said crossly, walking out of the kitchen up the passage towards me, shouting, "Adam, get into the bedroom now!"

Whilst undressing me, Mum said, "Your father and I love you very much and we want the best for you. That's the only reason you're going to Bright Side School."

When I was tucked up in bed April asked Mum, "Can I talk to Adam for a couple of minutes?"

"Yes, love, you can, but don't be long as I need you to wash up with Sean," Mum sighed.

April was another tall one in the family. She had long blond hair with beautiful hazel eyes. I would have to say that one of April's loves was buying shoes by the bagload. I can tell you she had about twenty pairs in her wardrobe.

April and I were inseparable, even though she did have a bloody temper on her. However, my jealousy got in the way if she went out shopping or went to the cinema with her friends.

With a deep breath, April started, "Adam, my darling brother, I know you're very upset, angry, and probably really frustrated about your school situation, but everything is going to be all right."

"God, you're just like Sean. Haven't got a bloody clue. April, this time next week I will be getting bathed and put to bed by Mr. Wilson, my new house father, who we only met today. How would you or Sean bloody like it?" I answered, crying into my mattress, as I never slept with any pillows due to my epilepsy.

"Adam, Adam, listen," April said, as she gently stroked my head, wiping my eyes with a tissue. "Would you like me to ask Mum if I can make you some fairy cakes to take into school on Friday? So you could give them to all your friends. Also let's do something nice at the weekend." I just nodded.

April kissed me goodnight, "I love you," she said.

"I love you more, April," I replied, feeling bloody hungry.

Friday was my last day at Land Field Grove. Nick, Clinton, Gordon and I were sitting in the school playground eating the lovely fairy cakes that April had made.

Clinton was feeding me as he suddenly said, "What did I tell you about boarding schools? They're horrible and very strict. My friend Ian went to one and he hated it."

"Thank you so much for cheering me up, Clinton - NOT!!" I responded half smiling, and we all giggled until we had tears in our eyes. I was really going to miss those three very much.

Most weekends were great, with the whole family all having fun playing board games like *Kerplunk, Mouse Trap, Buckaroo, Monopoly* and cards, or going for a walk across Putney Common, which we would do Sunday afternoons after lunch if it was a nice day. Putney was a brilliant place to live, with the River Thames nearby where we could feed the ducks. I just loved it.

This weekend was incredibly tough for me though, as I was very aware of what was about to happen the following week and for some time after that.

A very sad Monday morning hit me, as this was the day that I was going to start my new boarding school. When I was being dressed by my mum, the fear I felt was overwhelming.

Sean had been asked to take the day off school to come with us to help Dad lift me in and out of our van. Popping his head around the bedroom door, Sean said, "Mum, I'm going over the shops to get some sweets for the journey. Do either of you want anything?"

"No thanks, love," answered Mum. "Would you like Sean to get you some chocolate buttons and he can feed you in the van on the way, Son?"

I shook my head. I was in the lounge with April, waiting for Mum and Dad to take me to school, crying my eyes out.

"April, why does my school have to be so far? I don't like the idea of being such a long way from home."

April stroked my head. "I don't know why but Adam, Friday will soon come around and you will be back home again. Now stop crying, I love you very much."

"This whole thing is so bloody unfair."

Mum came into the front room with my coat and new school bag and said, as she put my coat on, "Off to school now. April, love, see you tonight."

April kissed Mum and I goodbye whilst saying, "Love you both."

'At least you will see her tonight,' I thought.

As we arrived at the entrance of the school, the butterflies in my stomach and my emotions were working overtime. The first thing we did on our arrival was to go to the reception office to get registered, and then we were asked by Mrs. Pointer to go to the medical office to meet with Sister Grey, who Mum, Dad and I had met at my interview the previous week.

We had to wait outside the medical room for a couple of minutes. Sister Grey then opened her office door. With a big smile, she said, "Hello, Mr. and Mrs. King, and hello again, Adam. Nice to see you all. Do come in and may I ask who you are?" Sister Grey asked, whilst offering her hand out to shake Sean's.

"I'm Adam's brother, Sean. Pleased to meet you."

Sister Grey was a stout lady with black straight hair. She also had a very happy manner.

The medical room was quite big and bright. It had many cupboards and cabinets. Sister Grey sat down behind her desk and said, "Well, Adam, welcome to Bright Side School. I hope you will be happy with us?"

I just held my mum's hand tightly whilst Dad, who was sitting beside me, said, "I'm sure Adam will be very happy here, Sister. He's just worried about the unknown, aren't you, Son?"

I nodded, with my stomach in knots.

Sister Grey stood up and came around from behind her desk and asked with a smile, "Can I have a look in your mouth please, Adam? Open wide for me, that's a good boy."

Sitting back down she asked, "Does Adam eat well, and is there anything that he's allergic to?"

"No, he likes all his food, and he eats everything. Oh, I'm sorry, Sister, I forgot. He can't eat rhubarb. It makes him feel sick, but he's not allergic to it."

Sister Grey said, "I would like to weigh Adam now. Sean could you sit him on the scales for me please?"

"Yes, Sister, not a problem," Sean replied.

The scales were large and on wheels with a big blue seat. When Sean was putting me on the scales, Sister Grey said, "Can I ask if you have remembered to bring Adam's medication with you, Mrs. King?"

"Yes, I have," as Mum handed Sister Grey a large, white plastic bag.

Sitting on the scales I felt very unsafe because they moved around a lot. That day I felt so unsafe about lots of things. When Sean was putting me back into my wheelchair, there was a knock on the door.

"Please do come in," Sister Grey called out.

I looked over towards the door to see who it was, because with every minute that passed, I knew that the time would come for Mum, Dad and Sean to go home and leave me.

It was Mr. Wilson. "Hello, Mr. and Mrs. King. It's good to meet with you again."

"It's nice to see you again too," Mum replied, shaking his hand.

Then Mr. Wilson said, "If you're finished, Sister? I'll take Adam and his parents down to the boarding unit to settle him in."

"Yes, I'm done with Adam for now, but Mr. and Mrs. King, could we have a chat before you go home, please?" asked Sister Grey.

"Yes, not a problem," replied Mum as we all left the medical room.

On our way down to the boarding unit, Mr. Wilson said, "I see you have brought your teddy bear with you. Many of the boys have them too. Does yours have a name?"

While holding it on my lap, "Snowy," I responded ever so quietly.

"Yes, you love Snowy, don't you, Adam?" Sean said, pushing me. I just nodded. Snowy was a white fluffy bear with a black nose that I had since I was born.

The boarding unit had a great big playroom, which had four large dormitories leading off it. The playroom was decorated in red-and-white patterned wallpaper and the carpet was light blue. It also had many big wooden boxes full of toys like cars, Lego, farmyard animals, soft toys and board games.

Every dormitory had six beds, each with a bedside cabinet next to it. There were also three big wardrobes. At the far end was a door that led to the bathroom and toilets. There seemed to be a strong smell of bleach coming from it, which I hated.

In the bathroom were two different-sized baths and three toilets, which you could place a wooden chair over to support us children.

Mr. Wilson took us to my dormitory, which was number two. It was painted in lime green and had thick lemon-coloured curtains with yellow flowers. Pointing to the middle bed on the right side of the dormitory, Mr. Wilson said, "That's your bed, Adam. John and Gary sleep in the beds either side of you and they are very nice boys."

Dad noticed a pillow on my bed. "Mr. Wilson, I don't know if we said last week, but Adam sleeps without a pillow. He also likes sleeping on his tummy."

"Thank you for telling me. It's important I know about things like that. If you think of anything else I need to know, please just contact myself or Sister Grey."

Mum then enquired, "Mr. Wilson, can I ask what you're doing about clothes, as I haven't brought any extra with me for Adam?"

"Mrs. King, please don't worry yourself about that. This evening after tea, Adam and I will go to the clothing stockroom to get Adam's uniform and everything else he needs for school." Then Mr. Wilson asked me, "Would you like me to put Snowy on your bed for you?"

I gave a nod as he continued, "Right, Adam, shall we go up to school before lunch to meet Mrs. Hanson, your teacher, who you met last Wednesday? You will see Mum, Dad and Sean on Friday."

As Mum and Dad kissed me goodbye I just cried, as Mr. Wilson pushed me up to school.

Mrs. Hanson was a tall, delightful lady. She had wavy blond hair and large, bright blue eyes.

My classroom was very big. It had two sinks on the right and toilets on the left as you went through the door.

Mrs. Thomas, our classroom attendant, was also very nice. She was quite short with grey hair that she always wore in a beehive.

Mrs. Hanson greeted me. "Hello, Adam. It's good to meet you. We are all very happy to welcome you to class B. Let's meet the other children in the classroom?"

I nodded anxiously. Mr. Wilson said, "Have a good day and I'll come to get you after school."

In my class there were seven boys who had a mixture of disabilities, but most had cerebral palsy.

After lunch, which I didn't eat a lot of due to my nerves, I returned to the classroom. Mrs. Hanson gave me a new grey tray that I would keep my class work in, just like the other boys. Miss then sat down beside me and said, "Adam, I'm going to write your name on a white sticker and put it on your tray. So, can you tell me which colour pen you would like me to write it in please?"

I just looked at her as she carried on. "Okay, Adam, if I point to a pen, you can shake or nod your head when I pick up the right one."

I nodded at the blue pen, and Mrs. Hanson wrote my name in large letters and stuck it on my tray.

Afterwards I was laid on a green carpet on the floor with the other children in my class. Then Mrs. Hanson put coloured bricks of different shapes and sizes on the floor with us. Miss shouted out a colour of a certain brick, shape or size, and we had to pick up that brick in the best way we could. I did try my best to join in, but I couldn't because everything felt strange and very frightening.

About twenty minutes before the end of the school day, we always had a story time. On my first day, the story that Mrs. Hanson read to us was *Little Red Riding Hood*. I don't remember a lot about it as I was panicking, worrying what my life was going to be like now. I would probably be going away to boarding school for the rest of my school days.

At 3:15, Mr. Wilson came into the classroom to collect Kenny, John, Gary and myself from school.

"Did you all have a good day, boys?" Mr. Wilson asked.

"Yes, thank you, Sir," Gary and John replied. I didn't say anything because I was very shy.

There were some children at school who were unable to speak, like Kenny and Max, another boy with cerebral palsy in my class. Their way of communication was with something called a Bliss board. The board had many symbols on with the word written underneath. Kenny would use the Bliss board by looking at the symbols with his eyes and Max would point to them with his thumb. The boys who required a board carried it on the back of their wheelchair in their school bags so it would be accessible to them at all times.

Before we left the classroom on that day, I heard Mrs. Thomas saying to Mr. Wilson, "Adam hasn't been to the toilet today. It's very likely because he's nervous."

"Thank you for letting me know. I'll put him on the loo right away when we get down into the boarding unit. Have a good evening, and Adam and I will see you tomorrow morning, won't we?" responded Mr. Wilson, looking down and smiling at me.

When we went down to the boarding unit, Mr. Wilson sat me on the toilet, and when he came to take me off he said, "You still can't go? Never mind, we'll try again after tea."

Back in the dormitory I met with the other boys. There were six of us. Kenny, Gary and John I knew already because they were in my class, and there were another two boys, Stephen and William.

Kenny had cerebral palsy. He was thin like a stick and very short, with black hair. Kenny's character was wonderful. He was always laughing. He was a wheelchair user and the only one that used a Bliss board to communicate. Like I've said.

Gary's disability was spina bifida. He walked with a bit of a limp, he was ever so small, and his left arm was tightly against his chest. Gary had blond hair which was cut very short, just like we all had to have our hair in school. He was always kind unless you upset him, and then it was very sensible to keep out of his way.

William had cystic fibrosis and he was in a wheelchair. He could also walk a tiny bit. William was one of the nicest boys that you could ever meet. He was quite tall like myself, with ginger hair and matching eyebrows.

Stephen also had spina bifida. He used a walking frame to get around school. He was a large lad with a round face, and he wore old-style NHS, thick, blue-rimmed glasses that had a plaster on the bridge to stop them from falling off, but it never helped because every time I saw him they were always broken. Stephen scared me a lot when I started at the school because he could be very nasty and cruel.

John was a short boy. He had brown hair and green eyes, he was a great lad, and there was something about him I really liked. John had cerebral palsy and a speech impediment. His sense of humour was fantastic and he could be very loud with it. He made me laugh a lot!

CHAPTER 3

The boarding unit had ten dormitories which slept up to sixty boys aged between four and eighteen years old. Each of the dormitories was assigned two house fathers who were in charge and made sure each dormitory ran smoothly to their liking.

My house fathers were Mr. Wilson and Mr. Campbell. Mr. Wilson was a short man who had a close-cropped head of black hair and was a little bit overweight, with a strong Welsh accent. He was a jolly man and he liked to have a laugh and joke but boy, you didn't want to get on the wrong side of him.

Mr. Campbell was very different to Mr. Wilson. He was more serious and quite strict on us. Mr. Campbell was very tall with a large stature, he had a long face, and his hair was grey.

That very first Monday evening I was fed my tea by Mr. Campbell. It was quite overwhelming. I was very unsure about the process and how it would happen without Mum or April because up until then that was what I was used to, except for lunch times at Land Field Grove.

'I wish I was back there right now,' I thought, as Sir fed me another spoonful of steak and kidney pudding.

Mr. Campbell wiped my chin, saying, "Adam, you're a very good boy for eating all your tea. Now would you like a piece of cake and a drink of milk?" I just looked down and gave a tiny nod.

At breakfast and tea times, our dormitory always sat around the same table that looked out over the school car park. In the dining room there were many tables for different dormitories, which meant there could be a lot of noise, but mostly you would just hear cutlery as talking was frowned upon.

Boy, I really hated that school. Being away from home was a very large reason, and having strangers taking care of me. Also, sleeping in something called a dormitory with six boys was unknown to me because I had slept in my parents' room up till then.

Before I was bathed that evening, Mr. Wilson and I went to the clothing store to get everything I needed for school like my uniform, pyjamas and slippers. Mr. Wilson left most of my clothes in the sewing room for Mrs. Green, the sewing lady, to put my name in them.

Our school uniform was a white shirt with dark blue tie and dark blue jumper, blazer and trousers. I hated wearing the ties or anything around my neck because I felt uncomfortable, as the movement of my head and neck made them feel tight and restrictive.

Our dark blue V-neck jumper had our school emblem on it, which was light blue and black with a white trim.

When Mr. Wilson and I came back from the store, he put me beside my bed and I just sat there looking around the dormitory very quietly, thinking to myself, 'God, I just want to go home.'

John, who was playing with some cars on his bed, said to me, "Adam, don't worry, everything is going to be alright. I felt like you when I started here. Didn't I, Sir?"

"Yes, John, you did. It's very strange for everyone at first," Mr. Wilson answered back, beginning to undress me for my bath.

Then Sir pushed me into the bathroom. As we passed John who was undressing, I gave him a smile. I became nervous and very, very sad inside as Sir put my brakes on my chair beside the bath, and as the taps were filling it I began crying.

Mr. Wilson got some tissue and wiped my eyes, saying, "Adam, Mr. Campbell and I expect you to have some tears during the first couple of weeks. It's hard being away from home if you have never done it before. Alright, let's get you bathed now, shall we?"

Mr. Wilson lifted me out of my wheelchair and into the bath. He asked, "Is the water too hot, Adam?"

I just shook my head as I splashed around a bit. Mr. Campbell was in the next cubicle bathing Kenny when I heard him saying with laughter in his voice, "Kenny, you know Mr. Wilson is better at your Bliss board than I am, but come on, I have to learn."

Mr. Wilson, who was drying me and putting my new pyjamas on, said, "Mr. Campbell, if you need help understanding Kenny, let me sit Adam on the toilet and I'll be there?"

I sat on one of the wooden toilet chairs in just my yellow pyjama top, strapped in to keep me safe. I heard Mr. Wilson asking, "Right, Kenny, what are you trying to say to Mr. Campbell? So, you're pointing to *play*, and the next word is *Lego*, and the next word is *floor*. You want to play Lego on the floor. Is that what you said?"

Kenny must have nodded because Sir replied, "No, Kenny, not this evening. I'm sorry, Mr. Campbell and I are too busy. Maybe tomorrow evening and Adam might like to play as well."

I nearly jumped off the toilet in fear as Mr. Wilson really shouted, "Kenny, don't you dare jump and put your bottom lip out at me. I said no," Sir said loudly. With that I heard a hard slap and then I heard Kenny crying.

At that point I felt very scared, because I was extremely fearful that children got told off with a slap. I never liked Mum or Dad shouting at Sean or April but this was a whole lot worse.

When Mr. Wilson came to take me off the toilet and to put my pyjama bottoms on, I was very uptight before Sir said, "That's a good boy, I'm glad you were able to go. Now let's go back into the dormitory and before I put you to bed, would you like a cup of hot chocolate and a biscuit, Adam?"

I gave a nod. Sir pushed me back into the dormitory when Sister Peters, whom I hadn't met before, came in and said, "Good evening, boys. It's time for your medication."

Sister Peters was a short, middle-aged lady with grey hair and blue eyes. She said to me while she was giving the medication out, "It's very nice to meet you, Adam. I hope you'll be happy with us."

As I gave her a smile, Mr. Wilson asked, "Would you like me to give Adam his tablets, Sister?"

"Yes, please," she answered.

Before I drank my lovely hot chocolate, Sir gave me two white tablets and a spoonful of horrible, thick, bright yellow medicine, which I had to take morning and evening for a long time.

"Right, Adam, let me lie you on your bed and I will be back in a minute to cut your finger and toenails."

Our beds were made with two white sheets. They felt very crispy, especially when I was put to bed on a Monday night. The beds had blankets, one cream and the other one blue. They also had a dark blue and light yellow striped eiderdown that Mr. Wilson or Mr. Campbell would take off in the evening just before our bedtime.

Once Mr. Wilson had finished cutting my nails, he turned me onto my tummy and the lights were switched off. I was left in the dark feeling completely alone and very tearful.

My parents and family were my life. I understood I was only away from Monday to Friday, but this was a gigantic thing to get my head around as an eight year old. You would think going home at the weekends would help me, which it did for some of the time. But school would be haunting me wherever I was.

Also, when I began at Bright Side, I hardly ever spoke. This was for two reasons. Firstly I didn't want to be there, and secondly I thought people wouldn't understand me. Therefore what was the point of even trying?

The next morning I was suddenly woken up by bright lights shining into my eyes, and just for a moment I thought I was at home. I suddenly realised I wasn't. I felt the tears welling up as I heard Mr. Wilson and Mr. Campbell saying, "Good morning, boys."

Mr. Campbell came over to my bedside and began to uncover me. He said, "Morning, Adam. Did you have a good sleep?"

I didn't answer. He then took me into the bathroom and put me beside a sink. As I sat there completely naked, Mr. Campbell asked, "Are you able to wash yourself, Adam?"

I shook my head.

"Why don't you just try and I'll come back in five minutes to see how you're getting on?"

I had never washed myself in my life before. I was worried and panicking inside as to how much of my body I could wash in five minutes and without water going everywhere. The more I thought about being told off, the more the water would splash over the side of the sink, as my hands would shake and the water would wet the bathroom floor.

I was still sitting at the sink when Mr. Wilson brought John and Gary in to have their wash. John, who was sat at the sink next to me, said, "Adam, are you able to wash yourself?"

I shook my head. With that another question came. "Adam, do you live far away?"

I nodded.

"Can you talk?"

I gave a nod.

"John, stop asking poor Adam questions. He's shy," Gary responded, smiling.

Mr. Campbell came back into the bathroom and said in a cheerful voice, "Look at all the water on the floor. Not to worry."

Then Mr. Campbell helped me to have a wash and he took me back to the dormitory to get me ready for school. When I was being dressed, I heard Gary say to Mr. Wilson, "I don't have any more pads left in my locker, Sir."

"Gary, I'm busy dressing Kenny. You're quite capable of going to the bathroom and getting some yourself," Mr. Wilson responded very angrily.

"Gary, while you're getting your pads, can you bring some back for me please?" asked Stephen.

"No, get them yourself."

Then Sir shouted very loudly, "Gary, Stephen asked you politely to bring him some pads. So just do it."

After our breakfast, I was taken back down to the boarding unit where I had my teeth brushed with the most disgusting, pink, powdered toothpaste. My God it was nasty!

Before going to school, we had to line up to have our hair brushed by Mr. Wilson or Mr. Campbell. I must say, on the first morning Mr. Wilson brushed my hair, I had a few tears because he also used the comb roughly.

On our way up to school, some of us would have to go to the school nurse's office to be given our morning medication.

Before Sir took me to class on that first morning, he said, "Adam, let's go to meet with Miss Corn, your new physio. She's very nice."

The physiotherapy room at school was ginormous, with sticks, callipers, walking frames of all shapes and sizes, and more wheelchairs than you could shake a stick at. There was also a green carpet with many children on, and they were having their limbs pulled and pushed like nobody's business! I looked on with fear and dread in the knowledge I was going to be on that floor quite soon.

"Hello, Adam. I'm Miss Corn, your new physiotherapist. It's very good to meet you. You will be pleased to know I haven't sorted a timetable out for you. So you can have a couple of days off and I will catch up with you sometime this week about the days and times for you to begin physiotherapy."

"That's great, isn't it, Adam?" Mr. Wilson said, smiling.

"Looking forward to catching up with you," she said, as she was walking away and giving me a wave goodbye.

Miss Corn had black hair that she wore in a bob. She was tall with a soft face, and like every physiotherapist I have met up till now, she wore a white smock top, dark blue trousers and black clogs. She was very strict, and I never liked that about her.

"Good morning, Adam, and good morning, Mr. Wilson. How are you both today?" Mrs. Hanson asked when we entered my classroom.

"We are alright this morning, Mrs. Hanson. Aren't we, Adam?" Mr. Wilson said, looking at me. I put my bottom lip out, beginning to cry.

Mrs. Hanson said, "Hey, hey. What are the tears for?"

"We've had a lot of tears since yesterday afternoon," replied Mr. Wilson, carrying on. He mouthed silently, "It's about H O M E."

"Adam, let's go and join the other children in the circle. We are going to do some number work this morning," Mrs. Hanson said, pushing me over towards the centre of the class.

My primary school education was very different. The lessons were kept at a quite basic and low level throughout my education. Daily we had to do things like watching *Play School*, playing different card games such as *Pairs* or *Snap*, playing with plasticine, or painting and things like that.

There were some days when I would have to work on something called a teaching machine, which had what I can only describe as two very small windows that I had to look through, and when I pressed on one button, different pictures would come up. Then I would have to press on another button to find the correct word to match the picture. If I was right the machine would buzz, but if I was wrong a red light would flash. Then Mrs. Hanson would know whether I had given the right answer or not. This was so boring even a two-year old could do this.

Another machine that I was taught to use was called a Possum. I got given this by Mrs. Williams, the technology teacher, who took care of all the equipment around school. She often came into our classroom to teach John and myself how to use it. Mrs. Williams was tall and slim with brown hair and she spoke with a very posh voice.

The Possum had a screen with all the letters, numbers and everything else you would find on a keyboard. There were many ways you could use the machine, using either a hand, foot or a head switch.

I would use a foot switch and the light would move along to the character I wanted. Then I would push the switch again and it would type it. That was the way I would do all my schoolwork.

There were times when we went to her room for a lesson on our own. Mrs. Williams would ask me to write short stories and spell words like *bat, fog, sat,* etc. I also had to do writing exercises like *The cat sat on the mat, The quick brown fox jumps over the lazy dog.* Also many more tasks like these, which I found difficult, but I did enjoy this work and it opened up a whole new world to me and the beginning of my education.

As I got a bit more used to school life and everything, I found the rigid routine that happened daily quite reassuring. It began with having physio between 8:50 am until 9:20 am. Then I was taken to my classroom and I would be given a drink of milk, and Mrs. Thomas helped me to the toilet.

We had to then sit in a semi-circle to watch *Play School* very quietly. After it had finished, Mrs. Hanson asked us questions about what we'd seen that day.

"So, John, what window did they go through on the program?"

"The round one, Miss."

"Yes, John, that's right. Good boy. What did we see through the round window?"

I put my hand up because I knew what I wanted to say, but I couldn't.

Miss said, "Yes, Adam. Do you know?"

I shook my head feeling emotional.

"I know, Miss," said Gary putting up his hand.

"Yes, Gary, what was the answer?"

"It was about clocks and the time, Miss."

"Yes that's right, Gary. Does anyone know what the time is now, the small hand is nearly on the twelve and the big hand is on the six?"

Unfortunately there was nobody who could answer the question, as Mrs. Hanson said, "The time is half past eleven. We will do more work on time this afternoon."

We then moved to sit around our large table as Miss spread some cards out onto the table, saying, "Right, children, let's have a game of pairs now. Kenny, do you want to go first?"

With a nod he guided her to two cards, a dog on one card and an elephant on the other one.

"Is that a pair?" she asked, showing him both cards.

He shook his head.

"No, that's a good boy," Mrs. Hanson said in a condescending way. Putting the cards back in the same place on the table, she carried on. "Adam, it's your turn now."

I pointed to the first card that had an elephant on. I gave Miss a smile as I knew where the other card with the elephant on was.

"Well done, Adam. You have won a pair."

When we had finished and Kenny had won the game, it was lunchtime.

At lunchtimes children like me who needed feeding had to go to the physiotherapy room to eat. This was because the physios liked to try and see if they could get children with severe disabilities to feed themselves. I found this difficult and very often had cold lunches. Also, I was taken out of my wheelchair and sat on an ordinary wooden chair, which was quite difficult and bloody scary because the chair obviously didn't have sides on. So being a wobbly bugger, it would frighten the shit out of me!

A couple of weeks into my new school, I had to face another unknown experience. Yes, our class went swimming one afternoon a week, and I hadn't been swimming before, and the thought of it really petrified me. I was being undressed and put into my swimming trunks and a pair of inflated red armbands by Mrs. Thomas. I was becoming more and more unsure as to what was going to happen in the water.

Miss Corn first got into the pool, and then Mrs. Thomas lifted me out of my wheelchair and sat me on the side of the pool, and then Miss Corn would gently support me into the water. My arms and legs would be flailing and moving around a lot and I would be making a lot of fuss and noise because I was so unsure. I have to say that even with armbands and Miss Corn holding me under my arms, I still felt very scared.

As my swimming improved, there was one day when she said, "I'm going to let you go but I will be right there for you." I shouted with fear.

"Come on, you can do it. If you have a problem, I'm right here for you. Alright, Adam, hold my hand and then let go of my arm and kick your legs. That's great, Adam."

Then I started crying.

"Don't be silly now, you are doing well."

Over the next few months, I got better and better at swimming and I started to enjoy it and be able to swim further and go a bit more on my own. In the end Miss Corn would be at the side of the pool, I would be swimming and playing ball with John and some of my other classmates, and I really loved it, and it became a highlight of my school week.

CHAPTER 4

We had just finished breakfast and I was looking out the window, thinking about how Friday can feel so far away a lot of the time, when Gary said, "I see the dentist is in the car park, Mr. Wilson."

"Yes, Gary, that's right. It's time for everybody to have a check-up," he replied.

I saw Kenny look down and shake his head. "Oh, come on, Kenny. You're a big boy and you like Mrs. Peal. Don't you?" Mr. Campbell asked.

Kenny kept looking down and I thought, 'I don't want to go either.'

"Anyway, Kenny, you're not going today. So you can stop worrying," Mr. Wilson said, taking his brakes off to push him down to the boarding unit.

'Please don't let it be my turn at the dentist today,' I thought, panicking inside as Mr. Campbell pushed me up to have my morning dose of physiotherapy.

In class that day and for some days after, every time there was a knock on the classroom door, we all jumped out of our skin with fear, knowing it was going to be one of us next.

I had attended Bright Side school for about eleven months now but time never made much difference to me, as my emotions and feelings were very transparent, not altering very much.

I was even aware that my parents had given them permission to cut my hair, my nails, sort out my school uniform and take me to appointments. I was expecting that I would have to go to the school dentist but not so soon.

My turn came on a bright and sunny Tuesday morning. We were playing just outside our classroom door with sand and water, which were in two separate large, raised, plastic tubs. It was so warm that day, Mrs. Hanson and Mrs. Thomas helped us to take off our school jumpers and roll up our shirt sleeves so we could play in the water and sand. I was playing in the water with Max. We had boats, cups and different things that we could try and grab hold of to fill up and empty. Ten minutes into my enjoyment of water play, John and Mr. Campbell came into class and out to where all of us were.

Mrs. Hanson said, "Good morning, Mr. Campbell. Morning, John. Did everything go alright at the dentist?"

"Yes, Miss, my teeth are fine," John replied.

My heart was beating fast as I thought, 'Please, Sir, go away now, don't say my name.'

Mrs. Hanson asked, "Do you need to take anybody else for the dentist, Mr. Campbell?"

"Yes, I do, Mrs. Hanson."

Kenny's face went white as Sir carried on saying, "Could I take Adam, please?"

"Not a problem, Mr. Campbell. Adam, take your hands out of the water and let me dry them, and I'll roll your sleeves back down, then you can go with Mr. Campbell."

Going along the corridor, Mr. Campbell said, "Adam, I understand this is your first visit to the school dentist but try not to worry. Mrs. Peal is really nice."

As I was exiting the school and nearing the dentist's caravan, the fear escalated inside me because I just wanted my mum, as she would always attend appointments like this with me in the past.

Mrs. Peal, our school dentist, was a short lady with straight blond hair and blue eyes.

"It's nice to meet you, Adam," Mrs. Peal said, as Mr. Campbell and I were going up on the lift. I just looked at her, feeling very worried.

When we came off the lift and into the caravan, Karen, Mrs. Peal's assistant, said, "Hello, Adam. It's good to meet you." I just looked at her, half crying.

Karen was a lovely and very happy young lady, with pink hair and a ring through her nose.

"Mr. Campbell, can you lift Adam into the dentist chair for me, please?" Mrs. Peal asked.

Sir picked me up and put me in the chair, saying in a harsh voice, "Enough tears now."

When I was sat in the dentist chair, she said, "Now, Adam, can you try and open your mouth as wide as you can, please?"

When I opened my mouth, she put a black rubber wedge between my gums to hold my mouth open. I struggled because I didn't like it one bit.

"Alright, just try to relax for me, Adam. Be a brave boy now."

'That's easier said than done,' I thought.

"You're doing well. It's going to be over soon," she said, examining all my teeth.

When Mrs. Peal had finished, she said, "Karen, I may have to write to Adam's parents to get permission to take out his milk teeth. Can you sort that out please?"

"Yes, not a problem. When do you need to know by?"

"Next Monday, if you can."

Sir was putting me back into my wheelchair. Mrs. Peal smiled and said, "Well done for today, Adam, and I hope to see you again next week."

"Say goodbye to Mrs. Peal."

I nodded with a smile, but I was feeling very down as I knew I would have to go through that all again, only next week would be much more painful.

In class before the end of another school day, I was sitting at the table finishing a painting. My hands were a mess, and Mr. Wilson came to collect us. He looked down at the table, saying, "Wow, Adam, that is very good. Shall we ask Mrs. Hanson if you can put that up above your bed?" I smiled and gave a nod.

Mrs. Hanson replied, "Yes, what a good idea, Mr. Wilson, and that way everyone will see how clever you are."

Then Sir carried on, saying with laughter in his voice, "I am also going to have to give you a scrub in the bath tonight."

Before leaving the classroom Mrs. Hanson said, "Can I have a word please, Mr. Wilson?"

"Yes, I hope nothing is wrong?"

"No, it's just about Adam." My ears pricked up as I was sitting away from them and praying I wasn't in trouble.

"I've taught Adam for the last year and he's a very bright boy. However, I would like to know if he talks to you or the other children in the boarding unit."

"No, I can't say I have noticed but I am aware Adam talks at home."

Mrs. Hanson replied, "I may have to talk to the speech therapist and see what she says."

"Well, do let me know how you get on. I might have a talk with his Mum. I'd better go and get the boys ready for tea and get Adam cleaned up too," Mr. Wilson said, looking at me, smiling and holding my painting. I gave him a small nod.

As Sir was pushing me down to the boarding unit I was thinking, 'I can speak, I just can't be bothered, to be honest.'

When we were back in the dormitory Mr. Wilson got two drawing pins, and standing on a chair, he said, "William, can you help Adam to tell me if his painting is straight, please?"

So William, looking at me and the wall, said, "Up a bit, Sir. If you bring the right side lower a little that will be fine, Sir. Am I right, Adam?"

I nodded. Sir got down off the chair and looking up at the wall he appraised it. "That looks great up there."

Mr. Wilson turned my wheelchair around to face William and Sir said, crouching down beside me, "Can you say thank you to William, please, Adam?"

Ever so quietly like a little mouse, I answered, "Thank you."

Mr. Wilson stood up and clapped, and laughing he said, "I think someone has been having us on Mr. Campbell. Am I correct, Adam?" I looked down and shook my head.

A few months later, Mum and Dad came up to the school for my first yearly review. They spoke with my teacher, physiotherapist and speech therapist.

About 3:30, when I was back in the dormitory after finishing school, I had a great surprise as my parents came down to the boarding unit to have a chat with Mr. Wilson and Mr. Campbell and to see me. I didn't know they were in school that day. I sat there quietly but feeling happy.

As Mr. Wilson took my tie off and put my slippers on, he said, "How did everything go today, Mr. and Mrs. King?"

"It all went well. Adam has come along tremendously since he started here a year ago," Mum replied.

"Yes, Mr. Campbell and I are very happy with his progress, aren't we?"

"Yes, Adam is a very nice lad. We just wish he'd talk more to us and the other boys. Does he talk at home?" said Mr. Campbell, as he helped John to drink a cup of water.

My dad laughed and said, "Adam never stops talking at home. Can I ask, is your name John?"

John nodded and said, "Yes."

Dad smiled and said, "Adam talks about you all the time at the weekends."

John smiled as Mum carried on saying, "Mr. King is right. Adam talks a lot. However, we spoke to Mrs. Pattern, the speech therapist, about a problem we are having at home."

"Can I ask what that is, Mrs. King?" Mr. Wilson enquired, walking away with Mum and Dad so I would be out of earshot. However, I was able to still hear the conversation even though I tried to make out I wasn't listening.

Mum said, "We spoke to Mrs. Pattern regarding the start of Adam's bad language at the weekends."

As Mr. Wilson answered, "Mr. and Mrs. King, at the school we have children with all kinds of disabilities, and some of them for whatever reason use that kind of language unfortunately. So I expect that's where he has picked it up from. What was Mrs. Pattern's advice to you?"

"She just said as long as Adam is talking, that's the important thing, and it doesn't really matter what the words are."

Looking at his watch, Mr. Wilson said, "Oh, it's nearly time for tea. Would you like to stay and have some with us, Mr. and Mrs. King?" I was nodding my head furiously as I wanted them to stay.

To my utter disappointment, Dad said, "Thank you for asking, but we have to get home so Mrs. King can cook tea." Mum and Dad kissed me goodbye as I began to cry.

"Don't worry, Mr. and Mrs. King. He'll be all right," said Mr. Campbell, pushing me out of the dormitory and up to tea.

That afternoon while I was being fed sausage and mash by Mr. Campbell, Mr. Wilson, who was also feeding John and Kenny, said, "Shall we all go for a walk in the park and maybe feed some of the school animals before you have your baths, boys?"

Our school was beside a gorgeous and very lush green park where we would sometimes go for walks after school or have sports days. Kenny gave a jump of excitement and almost knocked his plate off the table. John laughed, saying, "I think you can take that as a yes from Kenny, Sir."

Mr. Wilson was holding Kenny's head tight so that he could put another spoonful of food into his mouth. Unfortunately Kenny had real trouble keeping his head still, especially when he was eating.

Gary said, "Mr. Wilson?"

"Hold on, Gary. Let me finish with Kenny and I'll listen to you." Then Sir went on, saying, "Gary, I'm sorry. What did you want to ask me?"

"May I ride a bike or a go-cart, please, Sir?"

"Yes, you can, but we'll have to see what's in the store first. Would anybody else like to ride something?"

"Yes, Sir, I would like to ride a bike, please," William answered.

Then Stephen said excitedly, "I want to ride a go-cart, Sir?"

"Stephen, I wish you would remember your manners. But yes, you may."

"I'm sorry, Mr. Wilson, Sir," Stephen answered sheepishly.

When we had all finished our tea and made our way back down to the boarding unit, Mr. Wilson and Mr. Campbell went to the store where the equipment was kept.

It was quite a warm afternoon so we didn't need our coats. Our school had six animals. There were four small ones that were housed just before going through one of the gates into the park. Two rabbits called Bonnie and Clyde, a guinea pig named Sid and lastly, a tortoise called Tommy.

The other two were horses. They lived in the school stables in the park. Jerry and Puppet were their names. Jerry was a boy, his coat was a beautiful jet black colour and he was very tall, and Puppet was a bit shorter and she was a lovely ash grey colour.

Mr. Wilson said, "Who wants to feed the animals?"

"Sir, can I feed Bonnie and Clyde, please?"

"Yes, Gary, I've brought some salad from the school kitchen. Would anybody else like to feed an animal?"

"Can I feed Adam, Sir?" asked John laughing.

"Yes, John, give him some of the salad," Mr. Wilson smiled. I forgot being miserable and feeling lonely for an instant and laughed out loud along with John.

Then Mr. Wilson asked, "Adam and Kenny, would you both like to feed Jerry and Puppet when we get over to the school stables?"

I answered with a tiny nod, but Kenny gave an enthusiastic one. Then he carried on, saying, "I have brought some sugar lumps, so you can give them a couple each."

After feeding the small animals Mr. Wilson unlocked the gate that led into the park. Mr. Wilson and Mr. Campbell pushed Kenny and me along the path whilst John would be whizzing around in his electric wheelchair and the others riding bikes or go-carts.

At the stables, Mr. Campbell, holding the sugar lumps, said, "Adam, if you give me your hand, I can help you to feed Jerry."

Sir then pushed me nearer to the stable door from where Jerry's head was sticking over, and taking my left hand, he helped me flatten out my fingers, put a sugar lump on my palm, and supported me to put it towards Jerry's mouth. Jerry's tongue felt rough like sandpaper and he had large, gnashing teeth. I was scared that he might bite me as Sir was holding my hand tightly in place.

"Did you enjoy feeding Jerry, Adam?" I just nodded.

"Your turn now, Kenny," said Mr. Campbell, pushing him over towards the stable door. Then, like me, Sir supported Kenny to feed Puppet.

We always had about half an hour in the park and if there was time we would stop and kick a ball around. That was great fun if I was in the right mood. At times I felt miserable seeing other children in the park with their parents and I had to be at a place I despised.

Independence at school was very limited for me and some other children. Mr. Wilson or Mr. Campbell were not able to ask Kenny or myself if either of us would like to ride a bike or go-cart to the park as they were not accessible.

John's electric wheelchair was amazing. I would look at it with so much envy. I desperately wanted one.

Wishing for an electric wheelchair was all well and good, but it was not going to happen for me – well, not yet anyway! No, just a bloody pair of knee callipers came my way.

This was an everyday occurrence. For me, wearing the sodding things was purgatory because they were very uncomfortable. It was just like having heavy weights on my two feet. The two bars would rub against my ankles. The callipers were to stop my ankles from turning inwards.

Each morning before class, I would go to the physiotherapy room and walk in my frame with Miss Corn assisting me. The frame was tall, just as I was. It had a black, soft leather square on the top of it with an oval carved out so my torso would be able to fit into it and I would be strapped in, which seemed like a form of torture. (Oh, the pain!)

As I became more used to the school surroundings and slowly started to get to know some of the children and the staff, I gradually began the slow process of coming out of my shell. However, this had been noticed and suddenly my routine changed.

I guess Mrs. Hanson had spoken to the speech therapist, which meant I would be having physio and speech therapy every day now. My speech therapist, Mrs. Pattern, was young and thin with long brown hair which had the odd grey streak going through it. She was also a very happy lady with a wonderful sense of humour and I liked her very much.

The speech therapy room was large, with a table in the centre, and on the top of it sat three large mirrors. The two on the outside slanted inwards so that I could see my face from all sides at once.

Attached to the table, there was a wooden pole for us to hold onto while we were having the therapy.

"Adam, let's have you up at the table. Can you grab onto the pole with both hands, please?"

I would have to sit there looking into the mirror and try to grab onto the pole, which would take some time because my hands would be going everywhere. When I was finally in position, Miss would sit beside me and hold my hands firmly onto the pole, to still my constant movement and stop me from letting go.

Before beginning my session, she said, "Adam, I am going to put some honey on your top lip. Can you try to lick it off?"

I screwed up my face and put my bottom lip out as I didn't like it.

"Come on, Adam, try to lick it off for me. That's a good boy. Stick your tongue out and keep it out as long as you can for me."

I did try to do what she asked me, but it was just so difficult.

After she had wiped the honey off my lips, she carried on, "We'll have another go at that tomorrow morning, but let's do some speech now. Can you say *A* and *D*? One at a time beginning with *A*?"

I tried to say *A*, which was hard enough, but what was more challenging for me was pronouncing the sound of the letter.

"What sound does *A* make, Adam?"

"Aah," I responded very quietly.

"Look in the mirror and try to say *Aah*, as loud as you can. That's great, Adam. Now, try to say *D* for me, and let's have a very big voice. Very good, but please try to remember to pronounce all your words slowly because you can do it. I know you are able to. Can you say *Adam* for me?"

"Adam," I tried to say.

Miss said, "No, no, you can do much better than that. Shout *Adam* to the sky."

"Adam!"

"Very good, once again."

I took a deep breath and shouted as loud as I could, "Adam!"

"Wow, Adam, that was great. You're coming on very well. We'll carry on from there tomorrow."

The weeks and months passed and Mrs. Pattern would ask me to say things like *The Queen is quite quick at questioning, Tap on Trevor's tree* or *Mummy has a mountain of money.*

How bloody ridiculous, and every time I said something, Miss would say, "I don't want to see any dribble." Yeah right! I did a lot of dribbling when I was a young boy and it never quite went away.

Having speech therapy every day did improve my confidence immensely. My vocabulary and speech progressed too. Even though I spoke all the time at home, I began using more difficult and harder to say words, which also included a few more choice swear words. Much to my parents' disgust.

One evening, I was in the playroom watching cartoons when John began chatting to me. "You seem to be coming out of your shell a bit."

"Yes, but I don't like it here."

"I think that goes for all of us, Ad. Can I call you Ad?"

"Yes, of course," I replied.

With that, Middle of the Road came on the radio with *Chirpy, Chirpy Cheap, Cheap*.

"John, John, I really like this song. It's great," I said excitedly.

"Yeah, but Slade is much better, especially the one they have out now, *Come On, Feel the Noise*. That's just fantastic," John replied.

Having the radio on in the dormitory morning and evening was wonderful. Well, for me it was, because I loved pop music. John and I became good friends over our love and arguments about music.

Sometimes before we had our baths, John, Kenny and I liked to play with the Lego on the floor.

One horrible, grey Wednesday evening, John said, "Ad, I have a great idea. Go and ask Mr. Wilson to help Kenny and myself onto the floor."

"Why do I have to ask Sir every time?" I moaned.

"Just go and don't be such a baby."

"Shut it, John," I snapped back.

Mr. Wilson walked across the playroom.

"Sir," I called out, as he walked past us.

"Yes, Adam?"

"Please can you help Kenny, John and I onto the floor so we can play with the Lego?"

"Yes, but not for long."

"Thank you, Sir," Kenny pointed to on his Bliss board.

"Good boy, Kenny," he replied smiling.

"You creep, Ken," I whispered whilst trying to grab the bricks out of the box so we could try to make something on the large Lego board. Our hands wouldn't pick up or put the bricks exactly where we wanted them, which made this much more difficult and frustrating.

"The *Blue Peter* music has just started, so it must be coming up to bath time for one of us," I said.

John piped up, "Why don't we get more time to play?" whilst we were still lying on the floor and Kenny had just gone for his bath.

"I'm really happy, John."

"Why is that, Ad? It's very unusual for you even to crack a smile."

"I will ignore that remark. I start riding next week."

Mr. Campbell said, "Back in your chair now, John."

"Yes, Sir. I'm coming."

As John crawled over to his wheelchair and climbed back into it, under his breath he muttered, "I've been at this school longer than you and I haven't had one offer of a riding lesson. Don't bloody talk to me, Adam, any more."

"Have a nice bath, mate," I said, rolling about laughing on the playroom floor.

The next week, much to John's annoyance, I began riding every Tuesday morning if the weather was nice, as the paddock was outside.

Mrs. Young, who was one of the school physiotherapists, took us for riding. She was tall with dark brown, curly hair and had a loud, booming voice, which was very useful as she would have to shout instructions to us while we were riding in the paddock.

Many volunteers would come into school to support us with the riding lessons and help take care of Jerry and Puppet.

Tuesday morning at 10 am, I would have to go and wait outside the physiotherapy room for a volunteer to come and escort me over to the riding stables. Two of the volunteers that helped me to ride were Roger, who was an older man, I would say at least in his late forties. He was tall with a grey beard. Also Sue, a very jolly lady, who was almost as tall as Roger.

"Morning, Adam," Roger said, as he walked down the school corridor towards me.

"Good morning, Roger. How are you?"

"I'm very well, thank you. Are you looking forward to your riding lesson?"

"Yes, I am."

When we arrived over at the stables Mrs. Young said, "Hello, Adam. You know what to do first and you can ask for Roger or Sue's help."

"Yes, Miss. Roger, please can you take me into the stables to say good morning to Jerry and then help me put a riding hat on?"

"Yes, not a problem, Adam."

The school stables were large and very smelly, especially when you went inside. Before my lesson, I always said hello to Jerry as he was the horse that I would ride on every week. Roger would take my hand and help me to stroke Jerry's nose and face, then put my riding hat on.

I said to Sue, "Please, can you bring Jerry out of the stables and over to the mounting block?"

"Yes, of course."

When Jerry was at the block, Mrs. Young said, "Now, Adam, what do you need to do before getting on Jerry?"

"Check the girth, Miss."

"Yes, good boy. Have you asked anyone to do that for you?"

"Yes, I asked Sue, Miss, and she said it was fine."

Mrs. Young, Sue and Roger would support me to walk up the steps of the block. Then Mrs. Young would stand on the other side of Jerry. Sue and Roger helped me to put my right leg over. Miss would help me to put my right foot into the stirrup and Roger would push me up and slowly guide my bottom into the saddle. Once I was on Jerry, Sue and Roger would hold my knees and ankles to keep me safe. Then they walked around with me all the time I was riding.

Ben was another volunteer. He was much younger, probably around twenty-five or so, with black hair and a soft face. He would lead Jerry around the paddock by the reins. I was also able to guide Jerry, as I would have two bandages tied to each stirrup and then I could steer him myself.

Mrs. Young said, "Right, Adam, walk around the paddock a couple of times and remember to keep your back straight and your eyes looking forward please."

Riding was more of a physiotherapy for me. I might have loved it but boy, it was hard work.

Miss then shouted from the centre of the paddock, "Oh come on, Adam, get your head up, you know you can, you're doing very well. Right, let's have you trotting around the paddock now. Tell Jerry to trot on."

As I would be trotting, the sand on the ground would often fly up and hit me in the face. Also, my head would be bouncing around everywhere. Sometimes I would have to instruct Jerry to go over a very low jump.

After my riding lesson Roger would support me to get back to school.

Riding helped my posture a lot, so much so that I was made a saddle to go in my wheelchair so I could sit on it all the time. This was bloody uncomfortable because my back was very straight and what with the callipers on my legs and feet, well it was a sodding nightmare! However, I did enjoy my riding throughout my school years.

As a bright child, I was aware of a sense that the stuff that I was learning at my school was not quite the same as other children my age who went to an ordinary school. Especially because at the weekends, when I would talk to Sean and April, they would say about the things they had done in the week at their school. If they said that they had History, I would make up that I was doing the same subjects, and this started to get to me.

I recall a Thursday morning, Mrs. Hanson was opening the light brown, double doors to the large television set in time for us to watch another bloody episode of *Play School*, when suddenly I said, "Please, Miss, NO! Can we do something else?"

You could have heard a pin drop, and everybody looked at me with fear in their eyes, as Mrs. Hanson raised her voice and with clenched hands, she turned around and shouted, "Adam King, how dare you question what I do in my class?"

Very stupidly, I replied, even though quietly, "But I'm not, Miss."

"Just shut up and watch the last part of *Play School*, as we've missed the first bit because of you."

I was absolutely shitting myself for the rest of that day, I can tell you!

After school, we were all in the dormitory getting ready for tea when Mr. Wilson said, "Mr. Campbell and I need to talk to all of you after tea. But right now, can everyone leave the dormitory please? Not you, Adam."

Sir then shut the door, saying, "I don't like the reports I have been hearing about your behaviour. Why did you talk to Mrs. Hanson that way, Adam?"

Putting my head down and beginning to cry, I replied, "I don't know, Sir."

"Well, I'm appalled and disgusted with you, and you can stop the tears now. When we have spoken to everybody, you're going straight to bed."

"Yes, Sir," I answered quietly.

I was so pissed off that evening as Mr. Wilson said, "Listen, boys, Mr. Campbell and I have enjoyed taking care of you over the past three years. However, I'm afraid it's time for you to move to Mr. Jones's and Mr. Harwell's dormitory when school returns in September."

"Sir, are we all changing dormitories?" John enquired, feeling worried, as this was going to be yet another new experience for all of us.

"Yes, John, everybody is moving with you."

When I was in bed and half-heartedly pretending to be asleep, John said very quietly as he got undressed, "You don't look very happy, mate."

I whispered, "I'm so angry being put to bed early because of what happened this morning."

John said, "Well, I thought you were a bit of a knob. However, I know you're right."

I carried on, saying, "Also, I don't want to bloody move. Have you seen how harsh and strict they are on the older boys? God, why can't we leave school this year, those lucky bastards."

"I know, Ad, but we have another six or seven years left, mate."

CHAPTER 5

I had a fantastic six-week summer holiday, and as usual we spent two of them camping in Devon. Our family always went camping every summer. We just loved it.

We went to the same campsite most holidays. The site was gorgeous. It was about a five minute walk from the beach. It also had a small park where I would go and watch April, Sean and some other children that we had made friends with over the years playing on the swings, roundabout and slide. A lot of the time I wished I could have joined in with them.

There were times when I struggled with being made fun of by others because of the way I spoke or moved, which made me sad. Although there were times when Dad and sometimes Mum, if she wasn't busy, would come over to the park with us and they helped to put me on the play equipment. What I found amazing was Mum and Dad never treated me different because of my disability.

My favourite thing about camping, including sleeping under canvas, was the smell of Mum's cooking in the open air and playing games like swing ball, cricket or rounders just outside our massive tent.

Day trips to the seaside included paddling in the sea and building sandcastles with Dad, April and Sean. However, knocking them over just after we had spent ages building them was the best.

The one downside was that Mum and Dad always had to go to the same Catholic church before we could even begin to enjoy our holiday!

My wonderful summer holiday passed by far too quickly, and thoughts of starting senior school filled my head with fear, as this term was about to bring new experiences into my life. The only good thing about it was I would see John again.

Monday mornings were hell on earth for my mum. I can totally understand why she would dread that morning every week. My bedroom door opened.

"Have a great first week at school and I will see you Friday evening. Love you, Ad."

"April, just piss off," I responded from under the bed covers.

"Mum, are you sure you don't want me to stay and help with Adam?"

"No, April, love. You get off to school and I'll see you later."

Mum came into my bedroom with a bowl of warm water and flannels, singing in a very happy voice *The White Cliffs of Dover*.

She switched the light on and said, "Good morning, Adam, my darling. Are you looking forward to seeing all your friends at school again today?"

'No, I'm not looking forward to seeing fucking anybody,' I thought, very angrily.

"Shall I put on the radio, Son?" Mum then uncovered me to find me crying. "Oh Adam, please don't start this morning," as I started to hit, punch and kick her. "Adam, you have to go to school whether you like it or not," she yelled, trying to block my fists and feet.

"I hate you, Mum," I screamed, as I knocked another pair of glasses off my mum's face, which went flying across the room and broke, the right arm of the glasses coming completely off.

"Adam, you are such a naughty boy," she shouted, as she desperately tried to wash my arms.

The DJ on Radio One at that time, Simon Bates, played Leo Sayer's *When I Need You.* It didn't matter how sad I felt, I loved listening to the radio before school on a Monday morning.

Then I started pleading, "Please, Mum, can I go back to a day school? I will behave myself, Mum. I promise."

Giving a big sigh, "Adam, how many times have your dad and I told you that Bright Side School is best for you and you're coming on wonderfully there and you're going up to the senior school this year. Right, let me put you in your wheelchair."

The sweat rolled down her face. Then the real struggle began!

My heart sank as I looked out the front room window and saw the light blue school bus arrive to pick me up.

Mum fought to get my coat on, and on the way out to the school bus, I pushed my feet up against the white wooden door frames to prevent myself getting out of the house and onto the bus. She tried to kiss me goodbye but I just turned my face away. By this point, my Mum was just exhausted and in tears.

Being put on the school bus, I was told to, "Be quiet and stop the crying please, Adam," by Mrs. Martin, the bus attendant, in a very cross voice.

Mum waved goodbye and shouted, "Love you, Adam. Be a good boy and I'll see you Friday." I just waved back to her with a sad look as the driver pulled away for the brand-new autumn term.

Feeling petrified going off to school that Monday morning, it was bad enough that the summer holidays had ended, but more importantly things were changing this year. I knew that my two new house fathers, Mr. Jones and Mr. Harwell, were bloody harsh.

Mr. Jones was a tall, chubby man with brown hair and a bushy moustache. Mr. Harwell was also quite tall but he was slim, without any hair. Also, he wore round gold-rimmed glasses.

When I arrived at school, Mr. Harwell met me off the school bus, saying, "Good morning, Adam. Did you have a nice summer break?"

"Yes, Sir," I replied, wishing that I was still on holiday.

"We are going down to the boarding unit to see your new dormitory. All the other boys are there too."

When Sir was pushing me down the corridor and the smell of bleach was creeping up my bloody nostrils once more, I thought, 'It's going to be great to see everybody.'

"Hello, Adam. It's good to see you again," Mr. Jones said, as Mr. Harwell helped me to take my coat off and hang it in my wardrobe.

Our new dormitory was much the same as last term, but just a little longer.

Mr. Jones said, "Adam, you will be sleeping on this side." He pointed to the right, in between John and William. "And Kenny, your bed is the one in the centre between Gary and Stephen on the opposite side." Mr. Jones continued, "Have you any questions before I carry on?"

"Yes, Sir, I have. What time do we have to go to bed?" Stephen asked.

"Eight o'clock, half an hour later than last term. Right, let's talk about the rules, then you can go off to school. In this dormitory you're expected to do homework straight after tea. We expect you to come for your bath when we ask you. We will not tolerate being asked to wait. Lastly, there will be no talking after lights out. Do you all understand?"

"Yes, Sir," we all replied.

"Go up to school now and Mr. Harwell and I will see you this afternoon."

'Talk about fucking strict!' I thought, as I made my way very nervously up to school.

My very first secondary school teacher was called Mrs. Drew. She was tall with a soft face and a kind manner. I also met our new classroom attendant, Mrs. Davidson. She was quite tall with fair hair and she had a round face. I found Mrs. Davidson to be very stern but understanding.

On that first Monday of term I was wondering what secondary school was going to be like. I was still at the same school with all my friends but it just felt strange. Also, it was a totally different department to the primary school, and I don't know why but it had a very odd feeling.

The teachers looked harsh and unlike primary school, the toilets were in the corridor, which meant you had to be sure you went to the toilet in the break.

We all sat there in our new classroom, some behind desks and the rest beside our Possums, waiting for Mrs. Drew to begin the lesson.

"Good morning, boys. It's great to see you again and I'm looking forward to teaching you this year."

After she had taken the register, she said, "Now I would like you to write a short paragraph of things you did over the summer holiday, please. Call me if you need any help."

Our senior classrooms were a bit bigger than the junior ones. They were large, with light cream painted walls and a big blackboard at the front. Just like all the classrooms at school, they had windows looking out over the playing fields.

There were two Possums in our classroom that were on wheels. Now that we were seniors, we had to take them to our different classes around school. One of the Possums was for John and the other one was for me.

We both worked them with a foot switch. Mrs. Davidson worked mostly with Kenny and she helped the other boys that were able to work at the table.

I sat there looking around the classroom while I was thinking about what to type.

Mrs. Drew came over to me and said, "Are you alright, Adam?"

"Yes, Miss," I replied quietly, feeling nervous and shy. I then carried on typing about the two-week camping holiday I had in Devon with all my family.

I hoday to campi. It hot 2 wek. Mum cook fri brekfa every day was nice. I lik going besh and sea. Dad by ice creem for me. We go to fon far I lik it.

Spelling and putting words together were a massive problem for me at school. At times I would sweat with worry because my schoolwork was never like April's or Sean's.

Mrs. Drew clapped her hands and said, "Listen to me now, children. I am your form teacher, and unlike last year, you will be having different teachers for every subject you have, and I have a lesson timetable for you each to follow."

She handed us our individual timetables for our lessons, and looking at it, I realised I now had four different lessons a day. We all spent the rest of that week getting used to following our timetables and being at the right place at the right time. I was surprised to see some subjects on the timetable like Science, History, French and Home Economics (whatever that bloody was!). I had never had these as subjects before.

I don't know why but our school always had two swimming galas a year. The very first time I was entered into a gala was four weeks after I began secondary school.

The galas were always held on a Thursday morning at Charlton Swimming Pool. Our school would compete against five other special needs schools. The pool was very large and I had to race alongside children with similar disabilities. I would just race two widths of the pool because they were the only races that I was entered in. Which I was very thankful for, as the water was bloody freezing and not like our lovely, warm pool in school.

I wasn't very keen that first year. This was because I was put into the pool alone without a physiotherapist. This scared me, but I couldn't show my fear as I would have got myself told off in front of everyone.

The pool was large and the noise from everybody shouting and cheering for their own school was deafening and made me uncomfortable. Miss Corn put my red armbands on, saying, "Don't look so worried, Adam. You will be fine."

As I nodded my head, thinking, 'But you don't have to do it, Miss.'

Then I was lifted out of my wheelchair and sat on the edge of the pool. Sitting there with my feet in the cold water for a couple of moments, a sense of panic gripped my body.

Then Miss Corn was joined by Mrs. Davidson and they both held me by the arms, lowering me slowly into the freezing cold water whilst at the same time making sure I didn't bang my head on the side of the pool, as it was jerking around a lot and I was shit scared.

When I was put in the water for my race, there were six other boys racing against me. I tried to put my hand on the bar around the side of the pool like we were all instructed to do by the race official. I had a problem grabbing onto the bar with my left hand.

Then Miss Corn got down on her knees and helped me to position my hand on the bar and she said, "Try and stay calm now, please. You are going to be alright. Good luck and win a medal for the school."

As I heard the starting pistol go off with a loud BANG, I nearly jumped out of the pool. For the start of the race there was lots of splashing and we all started to swim across to the other side of the pool as fast as possible. My arms and legs were flailing about as I tried to swim in my own way to get across to the other side and win my first race. Mr. Richmond, who was our P.E. teacher – he was tall with broad shoulders, and large, muscly arms and legs – cheered me on from the other side of the pool.

"Come on, Adam, you can do it. I know you can."

Nearing the finishing line, I cut my foot on the pool floor, which I always seemed to do a lot in my school pool.

Unfortunately, that day I came last. I didn't win a medal for the school that year but the taking part made me very proud. Hearing everyone cheering my name felt great.

Now I would have to say one of my favourite parts about swimming was looking at other boys getting changed. We were always helped to get dressed and undressed at school by the attendants. However, John had just been helped to get out of the swimming pool. He was ecstatic because he had just won gold. So when I was helped to get out of the pool, I was taken into the changing room. It was large and cold and had the smell of many boys' odour mixed with chlorine in the air.

When I went into the changing room, John said, "Did you win, Adam?"

"No, I came last, and take that stupid smug look off your face," I said.

Then Mrs. Davidson helped John to take off his navy blue trunks. She said, "Can you wait a minute please, lads? I need to go and help William out of the swimming pool."

"Okay, Miss," John said, sitting there completely naked.

I could feel myself getting very excited inside as I sat there in just my navy blue trunks. I felt my willy becoming larger. John's body was lovely, with large red nipples on his beautiful white chest. John's fingers were curled tight and his smooth legs were crossed over, his toes moving the whole time.

"Are you alright, mate?" he said, but I couldn't speak. This was such a strong feeling and a very strange one too, as I had always thought about girls and that felt so nice, just like I was feeling now.

My God, he was gorgeous. It was the first time I ever felt that way and I was very happy and I so wanted to touch him. But I thought, 'If I get caught, I will be in so much trouble.' I also thought to myself, 'I don't understand what is happening to me, but it feels nice, just like in bed.'

Then suddenly I heard myself say, wheeling myself with my bare feet towards him on the very cold and hard floor, "Can I touch you?"

"What? Did you just say you wanted to touch me?"

"Yes," I said hopefully.

"Okay, go on then, but be quick!"

So, feeling hot with elation, I slowly put my very shaky hand in between John's legs and felt his willy and balls. They felt so nice and soft and a bit hairy just like mine. It was the most wonderful feeling and it just left me wanting more. John and I both enjoyed it and our willies became big and a bit of water came out of the top.

"You better go away before we get caught."

"Okay, mate. That was brilliant."

"Sorry, I didn't get that, Ad?"

"That was brilliant. Do you think we could do that again sometime, John?" We both smiled.

When Miss Bertram came back into the changing room and began to dress me, I thought, 'What has just happened? It was amazing touching John. But I'm scared and I don't understand what I have just done. I don't want to be queer. I don't want to be called names by the other boys at school. What would my parents say to me if they ever found out? What will I say to the priest at my next confession on Sunday? But why would I tell anyone? Was that so wrong of me?' The whole experience was really mind-blowing!

Mr. Richmond came into the changing room and said, "Well done for today, boys. Now if you're ready, those of you who can, go and line up to be put on the school bus so we can arrive back to school in time for lunch."

Then he shouted, "Adam, stop messing about."

"I'm not, Sir. My hair is wet and I don't want to go outside with wet hair."

Misunderstanding me, he said, "What is the problem with your chair, Adam?"

"No, Sir," shaking my head and saying, "My hair is wet and I don't want to go outside with wet hair, Sir."

I can remember this misunderstanding went on for quite some time. He finally walked over to me saying, very angrily, "Is that your towel, Adam?"

"Yes, Sir."

Rubbing my head very hard, he said, "I can't believe that we have spent the last ten minutes here talking about your wet hair." Then, pushing me out to the bus, he carried on, "You should be ashamed of yourself because you have held everyone up now. I'll deal with you back in school."

I just put my head down and said very quietly, "I'm sorry, Sir."

By the time we arrived back at school it was time for lunch. So I would get my punishment after. I received ten lines to do that evening, which were: *I must not hold the other children and staff up ever again.* Like I gave a fuck. I was on cloud nine.

One lunch time about eight or nine weeks into the new school term, Mrs. Davidson sat with me at the dinner table. On this day, after eating beef stew and dumplings, mashed potato and carrots followed by treacle sponge and custard, lots of thoughts started going around my head. Thoughts and feelings that I just wasn't used too mixed with all the new happenings in school.

Also that year, we had one teacher called Mr. Houston. He was quite short and spoke with a posh voice. His eyebrows were black and thick and he always wore a neckerchief that was chequered. On Monday afternoon and Wednesday mornings, Mr. Houston would take us for History.

I never liked his classes as they were so boring, and this was because he never included everybody into his lessons, especially the children who were very severely disabled like myself. Sir would often ask Mrs. Davidson to read us a story from the book corner. Stories like the bloody *Famous Five*, whilst he taught the more "capable children" in the classroom. This was so degrading and I just felt worthless, and why were my parents sending me away, and not Sean and April, only to be put to the back of the class and just being read to? I never listened to the stories anyway as they had nothing to do with the lesson. I would be watching the other children working like I wanted to.

Back in the dining room as I got more and more down and sad, I thought to myself, 'I don't want this fucking shit life anymore.' The tears began to run down my cheeks. I saw a fork on the dinner table. I grabbed at the fork very angrily about four times, until I was holding it firmly in my fist.

Then I pushed it very hard into my throat. Mrs. Davidson, who had just come back from putting my dirty dinner plate on the trolley, shouted, "What the heck do you think you're doing, Adam?"

"I want to kill myself, Miss," I said in a very uptight and upset voice.

"It's alright, Adam. Let's go somewhere quiet where we can talk."

So Mrs. Davidson and I went into an empty classroom and she asked me, "What just happened? Tell me why you said you wanted to kill yourself as that is a very big statement to make."

"I feel so sad, Miss, and I have done something, and I don't understand why I did it."

"Can I ask what you did that was so terrible?"

I spoke quietly and very fearfully, "NO, NO, Miss, I can't tell you. I'm sorry, I just can't."

"Well, Adam, if you won't tell me, will you talk to Dr. Trim about whatever is worrying you please?" I just nodded.

The next day I had to go and see Dr. Trim, the school doctor, which was quite embarrassing as Dr. Trim was a woman. She sat behind her desk in the centre of the room and the school nurse, Sister Grey, sat beside her.

When I was called into the doctor's surgery I had my gaze down towards the black, highly polished floor. I felt so embarrassed and worried.

Dr. Trim was a stocky lady with long, brown hair that she wore in a bun. She said, "Hello, Adam. What can I help you with today?" as she sat there in her white coat looking at me over her silver-rimmed glasses.

"I'm okay."

"Well you're not okay, are you, otherwise why are you out of class and in my surgery? Tell Sister Grey and myself what happened yesterday lunchtime?"

"I put a fork to my throat to try and kill myself."

Dr. Trim looked at me with a very shocked expression and said, "Adam, but why would you want to do that to yourself? You are such a nice boy, so tell me what is going on, please."

"I'm scared."

"Alright, and what are you scared of?"

I began to cry, as I thought if I tell her about what happened, they might have to look down there. God, I feel so shy.

"Adam, stop crying now and just tell us, or would you like Sister Grey to go out of the room and we can talk alone? However, if I ask her to leave the room I might not get everything you're saying."

I just shook my head and said, "I'm not sure what is happening to me."

"What do you mean?"

I looked down at my hands moving nervously on my lap and my heart was beating very hard inside my chest as I said, "It's my privates, Doctor. My willy gets big and watery stuff comes out of the top and it's not wee. I am so frightened and I don't understand why."

"Can I ask how you feel when the watery stuff comes out?"

"I feel nice all over my body."

"That is how you're supposed to feel, Adam. It's the beginning of puberty and everybody experiences this, so please don't worry because it is natural.

Dr. Trim whispered to Sister Grey, "Do you think Mr. Jones would talk to Adam about sex education?"

"I'm sure he would but I would need to have a chat with him first," Sister Grey replied.

"Would you like to talk to Mr. Jones, Adam?"

"Yes, I would. Thank you, Dr. Trim, for your help."

"Not a problem, Adam. I hope I have helped a bit and Mr. Jones will help you more when you speak to him."

A couple of weeks later, Mr. Jones sat down with all of us in our dormitory. He said, "Boys, I need to talk to you about sex education."

Gary and Stephen began to laugh uncomfortably, and I just looked over at John with his head down and eyes shut. I have never felt so hot inside.

Mr. Jones said, "It's alright boys, now calm down. I understand you are all embarrassed but don't worry, it's okay. Listen to me now please, lads," as he explained everything from having an erection to intercourse between a man and a woman. Then Sir asked, "Have you any questions, boys?"

"I have, Sir. Why do I have hair growing around my willy and balls?" Stephen asked.

"Well, that is your pubic hair and as you grow you will get more all over your body."

I thought to myself, 'I'm so glad Stephen asked that question as I wanted to know that myself.'

Then Kenny looked towards the back of his wheelchair. Sir said, "Do you have a question?" as Kenny raised his blue eyes up to say yes.

Sir took out Kenny's Bliss board from the back of his wheelchair and held it tight in front of him. With that Kenny pointed with his thumb: "Why, willy, get, top, wet?"

As Mr. Jones put the Bliss board back in his bag, he said, "Okay, Kenny," and continued. "That's called sperm and if your penis gets big and you have an orgasm then that is when it happens. Alright, boys, it's time for tea so John, Gary and Stephen wash your hands, please. Adam and Kenny, I will wash yours."

I did feel a little bit better after the talk with Mr. Jones. However. Why does it feel fantastic when the milk like stuff is coming out of my willy? Also, I can't stop thinking about John and I wish I could touch him again and also some of the other boys for that matter? I would like to talk to someone about this, but I just can't.

'Please, please, don't let me be queer,' I thought, as I was being fed cheesy potatoes with tomatoes on top.

CHAPTER 6

To my utter excitement, the school bus arrived outside my house around 6.30 pm every Friday evening and as usual Mum came out to greet me with a big smile.

"Hello, Son, are you alright?"

"Yes, Mum," I said, whilst Mr. Dickson, my school bus driver, got me off the bus and safely onto the top of the lift.

Then he pressed the button that brought me down slowly, level with the road. Whilst this was happening, Mum chatted to Mr. Dickson and Mrs. Martin, the school bus attendant.

Mum asked, "How was the traffic tonight?"

As Mr. Dickson took my wheelchair off the lift backwards with a bit of a bump, he said to Mrs. Martin, "The Southwest Road was bad, wasn't it?"

"Yes, it was awful, and that is why we are a bit late."

Then Mum took my wheelchair from Mr. Dickson, saying, "Thank you very much and hope you both have a good weekend."

"Thank you and you too, Mrs. King. See you Monday," they both replied.

Just before Mrs. Martin shut the door of the bus, she said to Mum, "How is Mr. King?"

Mum said, "Well, he's okay, except for the pain in his back, which he has had for a while now. But thanks for asking."

"I'm sorry to hear that, Mrs. King."

Then Mum saw my head go back to look at her, and very angrily she said, "Adam, I am talking to Mrs. Martin about your father. Have patience please, will you?"

"But I want to see Dad and April, Mum." I said.

"You better go," said Mrs. Martin, laughing.

"You are probably right. See you Monday morning. Say goodbye, Adam, to Mr. Dickson and Mrs. Martin."

As I waved goodbye, Mum began to push me up the path and through the white front door and into our lounge. I thought to myself, 'Why do people have to say *See you Monday*? I just loathe that bloody day.'

In the lounge, Dad was sitting in his grey and white armchair watching *The Sale of the Century*, one of Dad's favourite programmes, which would be on the television most Friday nights about the time I would get in from school. Mum took my black coat off.

Dad said, looking at me over his thick-rimmed brown glasses, in his deep voice, "Hello, Son. How was your week at school? I hope you were a good boy?"

"Yes, Dad," I said.

"Hello, Ad. How are you? Did you have a good week?" April asked, as she came into the lounge and kissed me on the cheek.

"Oh, school was amazing this week!" I replied sarcastically.

"Just shut it, you stupid boy!"

April and I got on great, and like I've said before, I loved her very much.

On a Saturday April would always help Mum to wash and dress me.

When April and I went into the kitchen, I asked, "Why was Mum so upset last night? I heard her crying."

"You should know why, Adam. It's because Sean went into the Army last Tuesday and we don't know when he will be home again."

"Nobody cried when I went away to boarding school," I said.

April said, pouring out some cornflakes into a bowl, "Do shut up, Adam. Sometimes you can really piss me off, because not everything is about you."

That Saturday, when April fed me another spoon of cornflakes, she said, "Are we going shopping today, Ad?" holding my head and wiping the cornflakes off my chin.

"Yes, I would like that, but I need to ask Dad for my pocket money first. Will you ask him for me, please, April?"

"No, do your own bloody dirty work!"

"April, don't be a bitch."

"Finish what's in your mouth, then I will give you your coffee and I'll wipe your face. Then I will take you in the lounge to see Dad and you can ask him yourself."

April then stood behind me and held the black-and-white striped towel under my chin. She then placed the orange cup in between my lips and began to pour the coffee into my mouth. With that, I jumped.

April asked, "Sorry, Adam, is it too hot?"

"Yes, and can I have more sugar?"

"What's the magic word?"

"Is it *now*?" I said, smiling.

"Do you want to wear this coffee or drink it?" she said with a smile.

"Okay, okay, I'm sorry, the magic word is *please*!"

After April had finished giving me my cool, sweet and nice-tasting coffee, she took the towel off from around my neck, saying, "You are aware we are going to have to clean the lounge before we go out?"

With a large sigh I said, "I can't stand cleaning, April. You're a girl, you can do it."

"Piss off, you bloody sexist pig! No way am I doing the cleaning on my own. It's our job on Saturday mornings, and anyway the exercise will do you good."

April pushed me up our cream-coloured hallway with its dark blue carpet into the lounge, where Mum and Dad were having some toast and a cup of tea and reading the newspaper.

Before she opened the lounge door, I said, laughing, "April, what do you think I do all week at school?"

"I don't know. Maths, English, Swahili?" April said, still laughing.

"No, my wonderful school week is an hour per day of exercise and that is so difficult for me that I need a day of rest."

"Oh, is my poor little brother feeling hard done by, now do I care? No, I don't give a shit! I'll hoover and you can dust."

Opening the lounge door, Mum asked, "What are you two laughing at?"

"Just Ad trying to get out of today's housework."

As I gave April a very dirty look, Mum said, half smiling, "You can get that thought right out of your head now. You know that's both of your jobs on a Saturday."

"Yes, Mum, I know. April and I were only joking around, and she is trying to get me into trouble."

Mum said, "Surely not, Adam. Are you okay, Son, and did you eat all of your breakfast?"

"Yes, Mum, I did."

I was sitting in front of my mum and dad, and Dad was still reading the newspaper. However, if you disturbed him, he would get a bit annoyed.

"Don't matter, I'll come back to ask him later," I said to April, hoping my dad didn't hear me.

"Yes, what can I do for you, Son?" Dad asked in a stern manner, as he put down his newspaper and pen which he used for the crossword that he loved doing.

"Dad, Dad," I said.

"Come on, Adam, spit it out now," he replied, getting impatient.

"Can I have some pocket money, please, and may I go shopping with April?"

Taking his wallet out of his back pocket, he said, "Three pound this week Adam, alright?"

"Yes, Dad, thank you very much."

Then he said, "Son, if you want something just ask me please, or next time you won't get anything. Do you hear me?"

"Sorry, Dad."

Getting out of his armchair, he stopped to rub me on the head and spoke. "Yes, Son, you may go shopping with April, but only after this lounge is clean. Your mother and I will get out of the way for you now."

I just smiled and thought, 'Shit, you have to work for every sodding thing in this house.'

After Mum and Dad had left the lounge, I said to April, "Why don't I ever get more pocket money? A fiver every weekend would do."

"I could ask Dad for you if you want. Anyway, what do you need more pocket money for? You will just buy more crap."

I said, "Just bloody clear the ornaments off the sideboard so I can dust it, but please don't drop them. I know how clumsy you are!"

"Did anyone ever tell you you're an arse!" April said, laughing, as she sprayed the polish onto the sideboard for me and put the duster firmly in my left hand, putting my left arm up on top of the sideboard and beginning to dust.

I said, "If you ask Dad for more pocket money for me, I will buy your magazines like *Jackie*, *Melody Maker* and another one if you want."

Whilst she undid the flex of the Hoover, she said, in a surprised voice, "Did you just say that you would buy *Jackie* and *Melody Maker* for me if I ask Dad for more pocket money for you?"

"Yes, and why are you so bloody surprised?" I said as I dropped the duster.

"It's just not like you. Now belt up and let me hoover so we can get up the high street," April said abruptly.

I shouted, "Are you going to ask Dad or not?"

Turning the Hoover off, April answered, "Yes, I will ask Dad, but not this weekend."

"Aww, why not?"

Putting back the ornaments, she said, "Just shut up and let's go shopping."

April put on my coat so we could go up the high street. Mum then said, "You need to put on your scarf and balaclava, Adam, please. It's cold out."

"Oh Mum, do I have to?" I said in a whiny voice.

"Yes, of course you have to, or you are not going out."

"Oh bloody hell, Mum, but I hate wearing my fucking scarf and balaclava."

Mum slapped me on my legs very hard and shouted, "Don't you ever swear like that again. Do you hear me, Adam?"

The reason I didn't like my balaclava was because of my movement. It would ride up and cover my bloody mouth, but Mum was more worried about keeping me warm than me breathing.

My Dad came into the kitchen, and he said to Mum, "What's all this damn noise about? I'm trying to read the paper."

When Mum explained what had just happened, Dad got very cross with me and he took me to my bedroom, taking off my jacket and throwing it across the room.

He said angrily, "Why do you never behave yourself, Adam? Your mother and I only see you at the weekends and you play us up, so why? If you carry on misbehaving, your mother and I will need to think about putting you into a home."

I shook my head very fearfully and said, "Please Dad, no, don't put me away. I love you and Mum so much."

Dad asked me, "Is it because you have to go away to school?" I looked down and lying, shook my head.

Then Dad stood up from sitting on my bed and with a big sigh, he said, "Right, you need to apologise to your mother now, Son. I'll call her?"

"Yes, Dad," I nodded my head very sadly.

"Rose, love," Dad shouted, "can you come into Adam's room, please? He would like to talk to you."

"Would he now?" Mum said, as she walked up the hallway and into my bedroom. "Yes, Adam King, and what can I do for you?" Mum said in a cold and very harsh voice.

"I apologise, Mum, and can I go out with April if I wear my balaclava?"

"Yes, Son, you can go out, but I don't understand why you make so much fuss about everything. You need to ask April if she will take you up the high street."

"Okay, Mum, thank you. I will."

As we were going up the high street, April said, "Why the hell do you make life so hard for yourself with Mum and Dad?" with the sound of cars motoring along the road, the smell of petrol having a good time inside my nostrils, and April pushing me, trying to avoid the potholes in the pavement.

I replied, "I don't know why I do it. I love them very much, but I feel really frustrated at times."

"Yes, I can understand that, Ad."

In a very angry voice, I said, "How the fuck do you understand? Are you disabled? No. Do you have to go away to boarding school? No, I don't think so."

"Don't be such a bloody martyr, Adam, for heaven's sake."

"Oh piss off," I replied.

"Just shut up, Adam, we are going into Woolworths now. These doors are so damn heavy, especially with a wheelchair," moaned April to herself, trying to get through the shop doorway. "I suppose you want to look at the records?"

"Yes, please. ABBA have a new single out that I heard on the radio at school and it's great."

"Anything else you want? Just to remember, you have three pounds and Mum told me not to let you overspend. So, the single is 75p. How much do you have left?"

"Bloody hell, is this a maths lesson?"

"Just answer the question, will you," April said laughing.

"£2.50?" I said, smiling.

"Wrong! You wish! Take off another 25p and you have what?"

Taking a big sigh, I said "Is it 2.25p, Miss? I've always wanted a maths lesson by the record counter in Woolworths, so thanks April!!"

"You sarcastic shit, what else are you buying, Adam, dear?"

"I don't know. Can I have a look around please?"

"Hurry up. You know this gives me a bloody headache."

"Alright, I'll try to be quick. What is that one at number six?" I said, looking up at the single records chart.

"It's Mud and *Tiger Feet*."

"What about number nine?"

"Number nine is *The Floral Dance*."

"NO thank you. What is number fifteen?"

In an angry voice, April said, "It's the Bay City Rollers, *Give a Little Love*. Now what do you want to buy?"

"Can I have Mud and ABBA, please, you miserable cow?"

"Now is that all you want, before we pay and go to Sainsbury's to pick up some shopping for Mum?"

"Oh no, shit, I hate that bloody shop."

As April paid for the records, she said, "Sometimes, Ad, I am so pleased other people can't understand what you are saying, because at times your gob is like a sewer."

"That's nice of you to say! Mum and Dad brought you up so well!" I said, laughing.

A tall man walked past us wearing a brown suede jacket. April said, "Can you hold the shop door open for me please?"

"Yes, love, not a problem. For you, of course."

Holding the door open, the guy said, "That must be a job and a half looking after him. Does he know what we are saying?"

April smiled and said, "Yes, everything."

"Where are you off to now?" the man inquired.

"Up to Sainsbury's for some shopping for our mum."

The man then kindly asked, "Would you like me to push the lad up there for you? I'm going that way myself."

"No, but thanks for the offer. Adam likes to look in the shop windows on the way up there," April replied.

"Okay, well I hope you both have a good day and maybe see you soon," the man said, gently shaking my hand and rubbing April on the shoulder before walking away up the high street. As she pushed me up the road behind the guy, I thought, "He's got a great arse!"

In Sainsbury's April parked me next to the magazine rack and said to me, putting my brakes on, "Now don't move. I won't be long. Have a look at the cost of *Jackie* and *Melody Maker* to work out how much they are together, so you don't get bored."

Whilst April was doing the shopping for Mum, I began to look at the mags to see if there were any good-looking boys or even young men on the front of them. But if I did want one, there was no way on this earth I was going to ask April. Because what if she asked me, why do you want the mag with the boy on the cover, don't you want the nice girl? Oh, why is this so hard?

On the way home from shopping, I was thinking, 'Tomorrow afternoon after lunch, I will go to the lounge with Mum and Dad like I always do, so they can read and write in my school diary.' This scared me a bloody lot, as my parents and I hadn't spoken about the fork incident last week.

Sunday morning arrived with a vengeance. The rain was falling out of the sky, bouncing off the pavement and the wind was helping the trees to sway. I waited by our open front door, looking out at the shit weather with my smart coat and bloody balaclava on.

Dad came up the path under his large red umbrella, and in a loud voice he said, "Is everybody ready? We need to get Adam in the van and leave now, otherwise we will be late for Mass."

"Alright, love, we're coming. Let me find my handbag. April, go out to your father and help him lift Adam into the van before he does his nut. Don't worry, love, I have your prayerbook."

"Okay, no problem, Mum," April said, smiling to herself, as this was a bit of a Sunday morning ritual.

Dad said, as April walked down the very wet path, "Come on, April, the boy is getting wet."

"Coming, Dad," she replied, holding a mac over her head as the wind and rain got stronger.

When April and Dad lifted my wheelchair into the van, I thought, 'Surely this weather is too bad and dangerous for Dad to drive us to church.'

After about five minutes, when Mum had locked up the house, she got into the van with her lime green mac on and a lovely coloured scarf around her head that was tied under her chin. She said, "April and Adam, pray to our Lord so we all get to church safe, and for your father to drive safely too."

As Dad drove off I just looked at April and smiled. By the time we arrived at church, the rain had eased off. Therefore I suppose God must have been listening!

Dad pushed me into Saint Martin's, our parish church, for 10 am Mass. The inside of the church was painted cream. There were eight beautiful stained-glass windows, four along each side of the church. They would catch my eye every Sunday, and I would wonder what bible story each depicted.

Also around the church walls were the thirteen Stations of the Cross in wooden carvings. The most beautiful and elegant statue was of Mary and Joseph that stood gloriously at the left side of the High Altar.

There was always the smell of old wood, incense and burning candle wax that would become stronger as you walked down the aisle to sit down on one of the many highly-polished, modern pews facing the magnificent marble altar that had a very large golden cross in its centre. It stood tall over Father Nicholas, our parish priest, as he would be saying Mass.

Most weeks, we arrived at church about half an hour early, as Mum liked to say her prayers. My dad put me in the centre aisle that was a couple of pews back from the front. He applied the brakes on my chair, then sat next to me. I never liked the silence of the church because it seemed to magnify the sound of my involuntary movements. As my foot kicked a footplate or my arm hit one of the metal sides of my wheelchair, that always echoed around the church. Dad put his finger on his lips to tell me to be quiet, which only made me move even more.

The congregation stood when Father Nicholas rang the bell by the vestry door for everyone to start singing the first hymn, number 152, *All Things Bright and Beautiful.* Father Nicholas walked slowly to the altar in his white and gold vestments and stole with two altar boys accompanying him. I always tried to keep up with the congregation, singing the hymns and saying the Mass. Mostly I was able to, but sometimes I was either too quick or too slow. Therefore people just heard my dulcet tones which would fill the church. I also have to say, sitting in church when you're a teenager can be difficult sometimes, especially if your mind begins to wonder off to a place where you don't want it to go at that time. An erection in your pants is not quite what you need when you're trying to pray, or at least look like you are!

I never liked going up to receive Holy Communion because the attention was always on me, as I couldn't open my mouth on time and I was never allowed wine, which I thought was very unfair! Dad always waited until most of the parishioners had received theirs.

He pushed me to the altar and he would hold me under my chin as Father Nicholas said, "The Body of Christ Adam." I replied "Amen," as I tried to put my tongue out for Father Nicholas to place the host on.

However it was very much hit and miss, because my tongue never kept still. I am surprised Father Nicholas had any fingers left after I had received Communion! I felt everyone was thinking, 'Why is he even here?' This made me feel very uncomfortable. After Dad had taken the host he pushed me back to the pew to listen to the final part of the Mass and sing the last hymn.

When we came out, everyone stood around talking and Dad stood behind me, holding onto my wheelchair. I think it was to make sure I didn't get away. Yep, like that was going to happen!!

Some of the parishioners ruffled my hair and said, "We heard you singing, Adam. It was lovely to hear you. God bless him, it's a shame."

I thought, "Why are people so bloody patronising?" However, if they thought I had a great singing voice, then who am I to argue!

But Dad said, "Say thank you, Adam, please."

"Thank you," I said, smiling.

I sat there watching a black bird hopping across the short green grass whilst Dad spoke to Mr. O'Malley, who was a short but quite stocky man with a grey bushy beard. He was very involved with the Church, helping with the church collection and supporting Father Nicholas to give communion sometimes.

Dad said to Mr. O'Malley, "The weather has brightened up since earlier on this morning. Poor Adam got soaked just putting him in the van, didn't you, Son?"

I nodded my head as I tried to say excitedly, "Dad look, Dad look at the two birds on the grass."

My Dad said, "Okay, that's nice. Quiet now, Adam, please. I'm talking."

Mr. O'Malley asked, "Where does Adam go to school, Mr. King?"

"He goes away to an all-boy's school from Monday to Friday which is boarding, which he hates, but it was one of the best schools for handicapped children, so Rose and I thought it was right for him."

"We are looking for a good school for Rhonda as well but it's hard to find one. Do you think Adam would like to come for tea and have some time with Rhonda next Saturday?" asked Mr. O'Malley.

As I watched the birds fly off into the trees, my Dad replied, "Yes, I am sure Adam would love to come. He likes Rhonda a lot, don't you, Son?"

I just nodded my head with a smile and thought, "Bloody hell, am I invisible?"

Then Mr. O'Malley said, "Don't you think, Mr. King, having a child with cerebral palsy is very difficult, especially when they have speech problems?"

"Oh yes, isn't it? It's the most frustrating thing in the world for not only us as parents but also for them, I suppose. Rose and I have many tantrums from Adam. They are mainly around his speech. If we can't understand him, well it can be hell on earth."

I was just sitting there looking around thinking, "For God's sake, yes, I am invisible," and I didn't bloody realise it was going to continue for the rest of my life.

Waiting to go back into church for my confession, I caught April out of the corner of my eye. "April, April, come here," I shouted.

"Adam, stop shouting now. April is talking to her friends so just stop it," Dad said in a very angry voice.

Mr. O'Malley said, smiling, "I'll tell you what. Why don't you, Rose and April come over to dinner one weeknight?"

Dad replied, "That will be great, thank you. I had better take Adam back into the church. He is having confession with Father Nicholas now."

"Okay, nice talking to you both and see you next Sunday. I will talk to Margaret about dinner."

"Say goodbye to Mr. O'Malley, Son."

"Bye bye," I said quietly.

Dad said, "Goodbye and take care."

April came over to us and she said to me, "Why were you shouting my name before?"

"Because I wanted to talk to you and ask if I could walk home with you and your friend Elizabeth? Please will you ask Dad for me?" I said.

"Adam, my lovely brother, I'm sure your brain is going. Have you forgotten you have confession? And no we are not waiting because you'll be hours," April replied.

As I was about to say something nasty, Dad asked April what was wrong with me, and when she explained, Dad said, "April, just go off with Elizabeth and we will see you later at home."

She kissed him on the cheek and said, "Love you, Dad."

When she walked away with Elizabeth, she looked back at me and stuck out her tongue. I thought, 'You cow!'

As Dad said, "Rose, Rose love, I'm taking Adam back into church to have his confession."

"Okay, Terry. I will be coming into church in a few minutes," replied Mum.

I got ever so nervous every time I had confession, but I never quite knew why I was worried about it as Father Nicholas couldn't understand what I was saying anyway. When Dad took me back into church, as he was pushing me to the vestry, Father Nicholas was walking up one of the side aisles towards us.

He said, "I was just coming to find you, Adam. How are you both doing today?"

"We are fine, thank you, Father," Dad said.

"Shall I take Adam from here, Mr. King?" he asked.

"Yes alright, Father."

So Father Nicholas pushed me to the vestry and shut the doors. The confessional box wasn't accessible to me because it was very small. Therefore I had to take my confession in the vestry, but there was no screen between myself and the priest, which I always felt was not right because other people in the congregation had this privacy. The butterflies started to flap about in my tummy when Father Nicholas began to ask me *yes* and *no* questions, which was very wrong of him because I wasn't given the chance to speak for myself.

Father Nicholas sat down in his large, carved, wooden brown chair next to me and he said, "Were you a good boy at school last week?"

I nodded my head.

"Have you been nasty to April at any time?"

I shook my head.

"That is very good, Adam," Father Nicholas said.

I smiled as he asked me, "Have you had any bad thoughts over the past month? Because you know they are very wrong, Adam, don't you?"

I just nodded my head, as he asked again. "So have you had any bad thoughts?"

I looked at the floor and shook my head. Father Nicholas asked me one last question.

"Have you played up your Mother or Father?"

I nodded my head.

"Was that over school, Adam?"

Once more it was a nod of the head. Then Father Nicholas stood and placed his hand gently on my bowed head and said a quiet prayer which ended with the words: "May the Lord absolve you from all your sins and bless you. In the name of the Father and of the Son and of the Holy Spirit, Amen," as I repeated, "Amen," very quietly too.

Father Nicholas said, "Adam, let me take you and put you in front of the altar so you can say your penance, which can be two *Our Fathers* and two *Hail Marys*."

Father Nicholas opened the doors of the vestry and my Mum and Dad were sitting in a pew just outside. When my Dad stood up to come over to take me from Father Nicholas, he said "Don't get up, Mr. King, I am going to put Adam in front of the altar to say his penance. He will be ten minutes or so."

Father Nicholas pushed me to the altar and applied the brakes on my chair and said, "God bless you, Adam, and ask for forgiveness. Give me a wave when you have finished praying. I'll just be over there talking to your parents." I smiled and nodded my head.

While I was saying my penance, Mum, Dad and Father Nicholas were sitting chatting, about six pews back. I must be honest, I was trying to listen to what they were saying, but I couldn't hear them as they were whispering. Anyway, I was supposed to be saying my penance, may God forgive me.

After I'd said my penance, I also said a prayer for Sean, as I had worried about him too. About ten minutes later I looked over at Father Nicholas to let him know I'd finished.

Dad came over, and as he wiped the dribble from my mouth, he said, "Are you ready to go home now?"

I nodded my head, then Dad took the brakes off and pushed me to where Father Nicholas and Mum were talking. Mum stood up and said, "Say thank you to Father Nicholas, please, Adam."

"Thank you, Father."

"That's fine. What are you going to do today, Adam?" asked Father Nicholas.

Mum replied, "I'm going to put the dinner on, and then Adam, Mr. King and I will read and write in Adam's weekly diary for school."

"Can I ask what that is for?"

"Yes, Father, the weekly diary is so the school and us can keep in touch with Adam's progress and the teachers and Adam's house fathers know what he does at the weekend."

Dad said, "Have a good week Father, and we'll see you next Sunday, God willing."

"Yes and you too." Father Nicholas replied.

When Dad was driving us home, I thought to myself as I was sitting in the back of the van, 'I wonder if Mr. Jones or Mrs. Drew have written in my school diary about me trying to kill myself? If they have, I will be right in the fucking shit! Oh, blast, I've just been to confession!'

CHAPTER 7

"Did your parents read your school diary?" enquired John, as he sucked his milk up the straw.

"Yes, it's a bloody Sunday afternoon ritual. My sister April washes up after lunch and I have to go into the lounge with Mum and Dad and sit there whilst they read and write in my school diary. It gets on my wick."

"Five minutes until the end of break time boys, so drink up please, John," said Mrs. Davidson.

"Yes, Miss. Sorry," John replied.

Then I heard, "Adam, Adam."

It was Stephen, bellowing my name.

"Yes, Stephen, are you just seeing how loud you can shout at me or did you want to say something?" I asked, smiling.

"Yes," he said. "Is April pretty?"

"Obviously. She is my sister, and more importantly, I'm her brother! Now will you belt up? I'm trying to have a sensible conversation here with John," I responded, laughing.

"Oh Adam, just ignore the sex maniac and bloody tell me, was it in your school diary about last Tuesday?" John leaned forward with milk running down his chin.

"Wipe your chin and I'll answer you, because it's going down your tie and you will get into trouble," I said.

"Thank you, mate, but will you just answer the sodding question, Ad please, before the bell goes?" John shouted.

"Alright, keep your bloody hair on! No, it wasn't in my school diary. Mum had a telephone call last Friday from Doctor Trim and she told Mum everything. That's the bell. I will tell you more tonight."

We had English for our next lesson with Mrs. Drew. As I was coming into class, I thought a lot about the meeting that was happening the next day between my parents, the school doctors, and some of the school staff. I began typing on my Possum.

Mrs. Drew came over to me and said, "Do you know about the meeting with your parents tomorrow?"

"Yes, Miss. I was just thinking about it coming into class and I'm very worried about it."

"Don't be too worried, Adam. We just want to get to the bottom of your problems, and I'm not sure, but I think you're having your school medical tomorrow morning as well. Alright, Adam, I'll let you carry on with your work."

"Thank you, Miss. Oh Mrs. Drew, please Miss, how do I spell the word *light*?" I asked.

"Right, listen now children. Adam wants to know how to spell the word *light*. Can we help him? Kenny, do you know the first letter of the word *light*?"

Kenny nodded his head and Mrs. Drew asked Mrs. Davidson, "Could you point to the letters on the top of Kenny's Bliss board please and tell us, Kenny, what you think the first letter of *light* is? Then I will write it on the blackboard," Mrs. Davidson said.

"Kenny thinks the first letter of *light* is *N*."

Mrs. Drew said, "Kenny, say in your head the word *light*. Can we all say *light* in the best way we can to help Kenny?"

"I know, Miss. I know the first letter," said Stephen, smirking.

"Well Stephen, tell us then," said Mrs. Drew.

"It's *L*, Miss."

"Yes, that's right. Good boy," as he punched the air in delight, the stupid twit! "The next letter to go on the blackboard is...? William, do you know the next letter please?"

"Is the next letter *I*, Miss?"

"Yes that's correct, William. Very good."

Gary and John were very bored with this bloody way of teaching and were talking to each other about the more important things in life, like Lego.

Then suddenly Mrs. Drew got very annoyed at John and Gary and she really shouted, "I'm sick up to the back teeth with you two talking and disturbing my class. Now John, give me the third letter of *light* and make sure you get it right or it's a detention."

"Is it....?" John said, very quietly and looking scared.

Mrs. Drew said in a loud voice, "Is it what, John? Come on, boy, give me an answer."

"Is it *G*, Miss?" John said.

"Did you say *G*, John?"

John nodded his head, looking frightened and hoping he had got the correct letter.

Mrs. Drew then asked Gary to give her the next letter.

"It's *H*, Miss."

"Yes, Gary. Very good. Now Stephen, can you give me the last letter, please?"

"Is it *D*?"

"No. Listen to the word *light, light,* T, T, T, T, what letter can you hear, Stephen?"

"I think it's *T,* Miss."

"Yes Stephen. Well done. That is right, very good boy. Now Adam, read the letters on the blackboard. Oh, do you need to put your glasses on so you can see it better?"

I hated wearing my bloody glasses. But like always, I felt myself nodding my head and saying, "Yes, please, Miss."

She put my brown-rimmed glasses with wire arms around my ears and elastic to hold them firmly on my head. "Okay, Adam, if I point to the letters, are you able to tell me what they are?"

Yes, I was able to read all the letters. I was twelve, but at the time that was how our schooling was.

Mrs. Drew said, "Now there is ten minutes until the end of the day. Your homework tonight is to write five different sentences with the word *light* in please. John and Gary, you two can stay behind."

While Mrs. Drew was out of earshot, John whispered, "Adam, mate, can you please tell Sir we are going to be a bit late?"

"Yes, I'll tell Sir you have been a couple of very bad boys and you're in detention for being cruel to me!" I said, laughing.

"Oh just piss off, you twit!" Gary said, a worried expression on his face because the words just fell out of his mouth.

Mrs. Drew walked back into the classroom and shouted, "Gary, did I hear you swearing? Adam King, what are you still doing in this classroom? If you don't want detention as well, you'd better get out now."

"Yes, Miss. Sorry, Miss," I said, quickly leaving the classroom.

On my way down to the boarding unit I began to think about what had happened the other week at the gala between John and myself. Yes I may have loved it, but I didn't bloody understand why I touched him. I thought it was fantastic!! I also really liked seeing the other boys stripped off. On another level it scared me to death. I felt very confused and frightened to talk with anybody about sex.

It can be great fun touching yourself through your trousers, but on the other side of that coin is, when you are a boy with cerebral palsy and you need every bloody thing done for you, privacy is not something that you can ever wish for.

I enjoyed masturbating naked very much but most of the time it was out of the question. At home and school, it felt that this was something that shouldn't even cross my mind.

"Did you have a good day at school? Do you have any homework tonight, Adam?" asked Mr. Harwell, taking off my school tie and undoing the top button on my white shirt as *Rainy Days and Mondays* by the Carpenters played on the radio.

"Yes, I had a good day. Thank you, Sir, and I have to try and write five sentences with the word *light* in for homework."

"Right, you can do that after tea," Mr. Harwell said.

"Of course, Sir," I answered.

When Mr. Jones came into the dormitory, he said in an angry voice whilst he was folding the covers back on the beds and putting our dressing gowns out ready for bath time, "Adam, do you know where Gary and John are, as the time is 3:50pm and they are not down from school yet?"

"Yes, Sir, they are in detention," I ,replied.

"Thank you. Right, go up to tea now."

On my way to tea I passed the two boys going down to the boarding unit and I just said, "Oh dear, oh dear, you two are right in the shit! Enjoy your next tongue lashing!"

"Go to hell," John shouted on his way through the doors into the boarding unit.

"Homework now, please, boys," said Mr. Jones, as we all came back to the dormitory after tea.

I sat at my Possum trying to think of sentences with the word *light* in. However, all I could think about was the meeting the next morning. Just as I was about to start typing, Mr. Jones came over and put my glasses on and said, "There you are, Adam. Can you see better now?"

"Thank you Sir," I said, whilst thinking of my first sentence to type, which was: *The light is put on at night, I have a light in my bedroom.*

After I had written five sentences, it was bath time. Mr. Harwell said, "Adam, can you go into the dormitory and go by your bed, and I'll undress you for a bath."

After my bath I was put into my pyjamas. We were allowed to watch television for up to an hour, depending on what time we were given baths. I have memories of *Take Your Pick*, *Ask the Family* and my favourite, *The Good Life*. But on Thursday evenings we were always allowed to watch *Top of the Pops*. I used to love it, especially when nice boys or men appeared on it, people like David Essex, Marc Bolan and little Jimmy Osmond.

Charlie's Angels was a massive favourite with some of the other boys, who would be glued to the large black-and-white television in the playroom. But at 8 pm each night Mr. Jones or Mr. Harwell would hear all of us say, "Ooh, can't we have another five minutes, Sir?"

As the off button was pressed, Mr. Jones said, "No, you can't. I'm sorry but it's five past eight and that is past your bedtime. Now, if you can go into the dormitory and stay beside your beds, Mr. Harwell or myself will come and put you in."

I pushed myself into the dormitory and Mr. Harwell came over to me and began to undo the zip on my bright red boot slippers. Then Sir went over to put Kenny into bed, and while he was lifting him, Kenny's hand accidentally gripped on to Mr. Harwell's glasses chain and the glasses went flying across the dormitory and broke. The dormitory fell silent and poor Kenny was so scared that he began to cry.

Mr. Jones said, "It's okay, Kenny, you're not in trouble. Nobody is going to tell you off. So calm down now and let's get you comfortable."

After everything was back to normal, John whispered, "Tomorrow morning, be careful you don't get a stiffy in front of the doctor."

"Fuck you, John!"

"Who was just swearing over there?" Mr. Harwell said, as he was making sure Kenny was all right and tucking him in.

'Bloody hell,' I thought to myself. How did he hear that? You're in the crap now.

"It was me, Sir," I responded.

Mr. Harwell pushed me to the house fathers' office. This was a massive room with a big wooden desk and many filing cabinets which probably had information about us. I sat behind the desk with my bare feet on my footplates getting colder and colder, as Sir didn't put my slippers back on.

After Mr. Harwell had closed the office door, he said to me, opening the drawer of the desk, "Are you aware what is going to happen now, Adam?"

"Yes, Sir."

"Put your left hand on the desk now. Right, Adam, what did you say to John?"

"I told John to *F off* Sir."

As my eyes began to water, I felt a very hard sting on the back of my hand and the two that followed were even harder.

By this time Mr. Jones had come into the office and he said, "Adam, what is wrong? You seem very unhappy, is there a problem?"

Sitting there with my throbbing left hand and crying, I replied, "No, Sir."

"Right then, bed, Adam," said Mr. Jones.

"Thank you, Sir. Good night," I said, as Mr. Harwell took the brakes off my wheelchair and pushed me back into the dormitory.

He turned the small light on and wheeled me very quietly over to my bed. When Mr. Harwell had put my chair beside it, he stood me up and sat me on the edge of the bed. Then he helped me to lie down on my tummy, and covering me up, he said, "Sleep now, Adam. You have a big day tomorrow."

As the dormitory went dark and I heard the office door click shut, John said as quietly as he could, "I'm so sorry, mate. Are you okay?"

"John, let's talk tomorrow, I'm not getting the cane again," I said, very upset.

6:45 am soon arrived. I felt the cold air as Mr. Harwell uncovered me while saying, "Morning, Adam. Did you have a good sleep?"

"Yes, Sir. My night was alright except for the snoring coming from John's bed," I answered, laughing, as Mr. Harwell removed my pyjama bottoms.

Then, grinning, John said, "I never knew my bed could snore. That is amazing."

Mr. Jones and Mr. Harwell were also laughing as I replied to John, with a smile on my face, "Oh my God, you think you're so funny!"

Sir then picked me up in his arms and whilst carrying me to the bathroom, he said, "Enough of this joking about now or we will be late for breakfast."

Mr. Harwell laid me on the table in the bathroom and began to run my bath. He lifted me in.

"The bath is too hot, Sir. Can I have some more cold water please?"

"Adam, the bath water is fine. Now just go under the water to wet your hair for me."

I was then lifted out and laid on a cold hard table to be dried. I hated that table. It was very high, and I felt unstable due to my involuntary movement.

When Sir was getting me dressed, I was a bit confused, so I said, "Sir, why am I having another bath? We never usually have a bath in the morning?"

Mr. Harwell lifted me into my wheelchair and put my shirt on, and doing up the buttons, he said, "It's because you are going to have your school medical today and you need to smell nice for the doctors, don't you?"

"I suppose so, Sir," I said, with my heart beating furiously, as I was anxious about the day.

"Porridge for breakfast, lads," said Mr. Harwell, as he was holding the very hot lid of a ceramic pot with a tea towel in one hand and trying to stir the very thick and sticky contents with a ladle in his other hand.

'It's always bloody porridge on a Tuesday morning,' I thought, as Mr. Jones fed me the first spoonful.

"It's alright, Adam, not too hot?" Mr. Jones enquired, preparing another spoonful to put into my mouth.

"Could you put some more sugar on it please, Sir?" I asked Mr. Jones as he was wiping the porridge off my chin.

"Can you please push the sugar to me, William?" Mr. Jones asked.

When William pushed the sugar pot over, he asked, "Please can you pour me a cup of tea, Sir?"

"Yes, just let me finish feeding Adam and I'll come and do it for you."

"Don't worry, Mr. Jones. Kenny and John have finished their breakfast so I can do William's cup of tea," said Mr. Harwell.

Breakfast time was always a bloody rush, and because half of us needed help with feeding and drinking, we didn't really have any time to talk.

While I was eating my breakfast I felt very scared about the outcome of today. After breakfast we went back down to the boarding unit.

When Mr. Harwell put my black and red tie on, I said, feeling ever so worried, "What time are my parents coming today, Sir?"

"Well the meeting begins at 10 am, so I guess they should arrive about 9:45 am."

Then Mr. Harwell crouched down to my height and put his hand on the side of my wheelchair and said, "Adam, listen we know that you are going through a difficult time, and we all want to help you. As far as the school medical is concerned, all children must go through it once. It will be over before you know it."

"Yes, Sir," I replied.

"Right, it's 8.40 am. Time for school. Do you all have everything you need for today?" shouted Mr. Jones.

I had bloody Mr. Burns for History that morning for the first lesson. 'Oh I hate fucking school,' I thought, as I was about to enter Mr. Burns' classroom.

"Good morning, Adam," he said in his deep voice, which came out of a ginger-bearded mouth.

"Sir, I may have to go at some point during your lesson because my parents are coming to school for a meeting."

Mrs. Davidson helped me to guide my left foot into my switch to enable me to use the Possum and to carry on working.

Mr. Burns replied harshly, "Yes, Adam, I am aware of that. Now be quiet and get on with your work."

All the time I was typing, I kept on looking up at the clock in the classroom, waiting for that dreaded knock on Class 4B's door.

Mr. Burns then said, "Okay, stop what you are doing and listen. Let's talk about our outing last week to London. One of the sights we saw was Nelson's Column. Can someone remember what the name of the ship was that Nelson sailed on? John, are you able to remember?"

Silence.

"Didn't you understand the question, John?"

"Yes, Sir, but I'm not sure what the answer is."

"Come on, John," I thought to myself. "don't get yourself into trouble, but more to the point, I don't know the answer either, so please don't let him ask me."

Saved by the knock on the classroom door. Thank heavens for that.

"Yes, come in," said Mr. Burns.

The classroom door opened as I whispered to Gary, "If you know the answer to the question, then tell John before he gets his arse whipped."

"Quiet in my classroom," shouted Mr. Burns.

Mr. Jones was at the door. "Can I please take Adam for his medical?" he said.

"Of course. Off you go, Adam. I'll give your homework to John, and I would like it in tomorrow morning," said Mr. Burns.

"Okay, Sir, thank you," I answered.

My whole body was shaking as Mr. Jones pushed me out the classroom. Going down the corridor, he said, "Adam, let's go and wait outside the medical room."

I was bloody shitting myself thinking about who was going to see me stripped, and how many people would be there.

In the medical room, I was aware that my parents and six others, Doctor Trim, Doctor Riga, Mrs. Drew, Mr. Harwell, Sister Peters and Sister Grey, were all talking about me. I felt nervous as I would most likely have to undress and lie on the couch behind the screen and I didn't like the thought of that at all.

Doctor Trim and Doctor Riga sat at their desk in white coats. Doctor Riga had straight, shoulder-length black hair, green eyes, and a narrow but kindly face. She was also quite skinny. We only saw Doctor Riga once a year, for a check-up and for our school medical. Doctor Trim saw us more on a regular basis, especially if we were ill in school or we had a problem that needed urgent attention.

Mr. Jones then pushed my wheelchair over on the other side of the room next to my Mum and Dad. After kissing me, my Dad whispered as he was ruffling my hair, "Don't look so worried, Son. It's going to be alright, I promise you."

Doctor Riga said, "Good morning, Adam. I haven't seen you for a long time. How have you been?"

"I am alright, thank you, Doctor."

"Am I correct, but did you say, *I am alright, thank you, Doctor*?"

I nodded my head and smiled. It was nice that she made an effort to understand me.

Doctor Trim then said, "It's nice to see you, Adam. This must be quite daunting for you with all these people in the room, so I'm going to ask some people to leave in a minute, but firstly, we have been talking about what happened three weeks ago and why you tried to harm yourself. Can I ask, are you unhappy at school, and I don't mean if you like it or not?"

I looked over at my Mum as she said, "Don't look at me, Adam. You have been asked a question. Now answer it please."

So, absolutely scared out of my mind, I said, "Doctor Trim, it's like I told you before. I'm still unsure of what is happening to my body?" with a bomb going off inside my head as I thought, 'My parents are going to explode.' I went on to say, "I'm still very worried about the conversation we had."

"Do you mean about sex and what's happening to your body?" Doctor Trim responded. I nodded my head very gingerly, because I was aware of what was coming and I thought, 'Oh shit,' because this subject was an absolute no-no as far as my parents were concerned.

Then Doctor Trim asked, "Mr. Jones, did you have a talk with Adam about puberty and the changes to his body?"

"Yes. I spoke to all the boys in my dormitory regarding everything on that subject. I thought Adam was alright with all that," Mr. Jones replied.

My mum became uncomfortable and quite angry, saying, "I am not happy to learn that my son has been spoken to about this subject, as I'm not comfortable with Adam being taught or spoken to about things like that at the age he is, or any age in fact. No disabled child of mine should be aware of that kind of information. It's disgusting."

Dad said to Mum, "You need to calm down, Rose. Adam was just answering Doctor Trim's question."

As Mum sat back down she said, "I'm very, very sorry about my outburst, but I just want to protect my son." Mum held Dad's hand.

Doctor Riga said, "Please don't worry, Mrs. King. It's totally understandable that you reacted the way you did. However, we must be aware of Adam's feelings, whatever they may be."

Mum then asked, "Do the children have sex education in school?"

Mrs. Drew replied, "Not as such, Mrs. King, because we aren't able to offer sex education at the school, as it would be inappropriate for some of the children."

I sat there thinking, 'I hope this whole bloody thing will be over soon.' I felt like shit.

Doctor Riga then said, "Okay, can I ask Mrs. Drew and Mr. Harwell to leave the room please? Doctor Trim and I would like to examine Adam. Mr. Jones, could you undress Adam and lay him up on the couch for us, please?"

Mr. Jones came over and took the brakes off my wheelchair. I held my right arm out towards my Mum and put my bottom lip over my top lip as I was about to cry.

Mum said, "Come on, Adam. Don't be silly. The doctors are just going to have a look at you and your dad and I will still be here afterwards."

Mr. Jones pushed me behind the green curtains, and he stripped me naked and lifted me onto the couch. 'Please don't let me have an erection,' I thought as I was lying there. I was given a thorough examination, which I found uncomfortable and bloody embarrassing.

Afterwards, when I was being dressed, I heard Sister Grey say, "Well Mr. and Mrs. King, Adam might have cerebral palsy, but his sexual organs work the same way as everybody's, and I understand that may be difficult for you to accept."

Mum replied, "Yes, you're probably right Sister. But Adam is our baby, and Mr. King and I don't approve of him being taught sex education."

Immediately after it was all over, I felt happy that I was healthy, but I didn't understand why my parents were making such a big deal about sex. After a long morning of meetings, I got back up to school in time for our lunch break. John was sitting in the lobby just outside the classrooms.

As I approached him, I said very excitedly, "John, John, I'm going to be assessed for an electric wheelchair. Isn't that fantastic?"

"Whose bloody idea was that? You'll be a crap driver, and why would they do that to the school?"

"I don't care what you think? I'm so happy I might get one."

"Anyway, did you have to strip off for the doctors then?"

"What do you bloody think? It was my school medical."

"Oh shit. I've got mine next week, so that means I will be asked to undress," said John, nervously.

"What the hell are you worrying about? Stop being such a big baby. It's only about twenty minutes that the doctors have you stripped for."

"Thanks, Adam, for saying that. You're the one that comes into school crying on a Monday morning."

"Piss off. I hope Doctor Riga twists your bollocks off!!" I replied, laughing.

"My God, you're a lovely friend, Adam. Thank you so much for those comforting words," John responded with a smile.

"At least your parents will understand about your sex life," I said, quite angrily.

John asked with a puzzled look, "Why the hell were you talking about your sex life in the medical?"

"Doctor Trim and I spoke about it a few weeks back, and she asked me if everything was alright. I told her I was worried about my dick getting big and wet, which she spoke about in front of Mum and Dad, and they went completely doo-lally. I just wish my parents were like yours."

"Yeah, I have no problem about that with my mum and dad. They're very cool with everything. I'm lucky. I know."

"Yes you are, mate, and I have got a bloody large fight in front of me," I said.

Oh why am I Catholic? It makes my life so damn hard.

CHAPTER 8

My thirteenth birthday was fast approaching and my parents were throwing me a party where I was allowed to invite some of my friends. To add to this good news, I had also been told I had passed my electric wheelchair assessment.

One night whilst we were doing our homework in our dormitory, I asked everybody, "Would you all like to come to my birthday party on the 12th of March?"

"Will there be girls there, Ad?" Stephen asked.

"You are bloody obsessed with girls. Anyway, there will be. My lovely girlfriend will be coming. Also my mum and sister April, and April is right out of your league, mate!" I replied.

William asked quietly, "What's your girlfriend's name, Ad?"

"Her name is Rhonda. We met at Church," I replied.

Then John's face went green with envy as Gary said, "Oh, we get to meet your girlfriend! What time is the party and where is it?"

"It's at my house between 5 and 8 pm, and I get to choose the music before you all complain."

Mr. Jones shouted, "Enough talking now boys, and get on with your work."

I had Maths homework that evening, which included exciting questions like *What is 6+4?* and W*hat is 96-30?* I did enjoy Maths a lot, but sometimes Miss Farmstead, our Maths teacher, would give me difficult work and this evening was beginning to feel like one of those times.

I put up my hand. "Sir, help me please?"

"Just a minute, Adam. Let me finish with Kenny and I'll be over," Mr. Harwell said.

As I was trying to take away 30 from 300 on my fingers and toes, I turned to John who was working next to me and huffed, "Sod this," stomping my foot.

"Harwell is coming to help you now, so stop complaining like a wimp," John laughed.

"Oh thank you, you sod!" I answered, looking over my glasses.

Sir then came over and peered at the paper that had been propped up on a stand beside me before inspecting the work that I'd typed up on my Possum. "What's 300 take away 30? Come on, Adam, just think about it."

I slowly typed out 250 on my Possum, really trying to concentrate.

Impatiently he shouted, "No, that is wrong. It's not 250. Adam, you are not moving until you get this sum correct, even if you have to miss watching television tonight."

"Yes, Sir," I said, thinking, 'You fucking bastard,' as he walked away.

I sat in front of my Possum trying everything to work out this bloody sum in my head, but it just wouldn't come to me. Then half an hour later, with the *Magic Roundabout* theme tune playing in my ears, I finally prayed that I had the right answer.

Mr. Jones asked, "Have you finished your Maths homework, Adam? Let's see, 270. Yes, that's right at last. Good boy."

'Thank God for that,' I thought, as Sir went on to say, "Now go into the dormitory and start undressing for a bath, please."

As I began to prepare for my bath that evening, Gary, who was drying himself with a yellow-and-black striped towel next to me, said, "Ad, what would you like for your birthday, mate?"

"I'm not sure." I knew what I wanted the most, and that was records, although Mum and Dad would probably try and persuade me to get some new, smart clothes for church.

"All your money!" I answered, laughing.

"Piss off, Ad. So you can spend it all on this new girlfriend?" he smirked, putting on his gingham dressing gown. "Is that what it's like to be Catholic? I didn't realise that you were allowed to chase girls around the church!"

"I wish," I smiled, thinking that I would like to chase John around the altar. "The only saving grace are a few of the catchier hymns," I said. "Being Catholic is so difficult."

"Well at least there are girls there," Gary said, as he walked out of the dormitory to go and watch one of my favourites, *Opportunity Knocks*.

I loved that bloody programme, but I was in the dormitory struggling to undress myself, as the physiotherapists had told Mr. Jones and Mr. Harwell to try and encourage me to do this as much as I was able to do so alone. So there I was, topless and without any callipers or socks on, bloody frustrated and stuck on the top button of my trousers. The angrier I got at the sodding button the more difficult it became for me. Mr. Jones then came into the dormitory to see if I'd finished undressing.

I said, "Sir, I'm stuck."

"Well, Adam, I know it's hard, but you need to become more independent, and don't you think that would be better than Mr. Harwell or I do it for you?" Mr. Jones said, reluctantly helping me to undo the top button on my trousers.

I just nodded and kept on wrestling with my clothes. By the time I'd undressed and had a bath it was time for bed. So no bloody recreational time for me, also not even being allowed to receive my once-a-week phone call from Mum. That really pissed me off because that once-a-week telephone call from our parents was important to all of us.

The next morning our first lesson was Maths. Miss Farmstead said, as she was marking the homework, "Adam, you have done well with your Maths homework this week. You have got 7 out of 10."

"Thank you, Miss," I replied, typing out the seven times table on my Possum. I just found the times table sodding difficult. Oh not tens. They were piss easy!

Still trying to get the seven times table right in my bloody head, I looked over at John, who was working away on the other side of the classroom, and I thought, 'I know you can't brush your hair, mate, but you could fucking ask someone to do it for you. It's a bloody mess. You're just lucky you're so hot you are able to pull that disaster off!!'

Since looking at John in Maths, I had felt very sexy. Therefore throughout my lunch time, I kept looking at the clock because I was so desperate for a wank, and I only had ten minutes before physio.

Mrs. Davidson asked, "Do you need to go to the toilet, Adam?"

"No, Miss," I replied.

My willy was very erect, and I was trying to rush as fast as possible down the corridor and into the bogs for a good wank through my trousers.

Masturbating naked is wonderful, and that isn't going to happen anytime soon, well not until I have learned to fucking undress myself and have a private space where I will be left alone.

Also, sharing a dormitory with six boys can be embarrassing, especially when you are trying to keep a secret about your sexuality and the obsession you have with another boy. Therefore it doesn't matter how hard you might desperately want to keep something discreet, or in my case, someone. It's just ruddy impossible.

I was going very fast down the long school corridor, which was painted cream with pictures of assorted fruits, flowers and countryside. My school's taste in art was non-existent!! "Slow down, Adam, please," I heard Mr. Burns say as he walked past me.

"Yes, Sir," I replied, as I thought, 'God Burns, you do have a great arse and come on, Adam, get to the toilet or you'll never have enough time.'

As I was turning left to go into the loo and sweating like a pig because time wasn't on my side, I heard a loud grunt, but I was just about ten feet from the toilet door with excitement going through my body so I ignored it. But then I heard it again, only this time it was two grunts and a hard kick on my chair with a great big giggle!

As I looked behind me thinking, 'Fuck, why now?' I said, "Oh Kenny, you bastard! I'm about to go for a wank. What do you want?"

Kenny nodded with a serious expression on his face. I knew he wanted to talk to me. Oh fuck! We only had five minutes until we had to be in physio so I knew I had missed my chance. It took me longer to understand Kenny but he looked worried, his bottom lip was sticking out.

I wanted to make sure that he was okay but we didn't have time, so I turned towards him and said, "Don't worry. Talk more later, Ken."

Kenny looked at me and slowly nodded his head with a slight smile to say, "Alright," as we made our way down the corridor towards physio and further away from the privacy of the toilet.

"Hello, boys. You're a bit late this afternoon," Miss Corn grumbled.

"Sorry, Miss."

"Right, Adam, if I undo your lap belt can you get out of your chair? Don't take off your callipers today, Adam, because I'm going to walk with you," said Miss Corn, as she helped Kenny to take off his socks and shoes and undid his lap belt so she could support him down to the floor.

The best thing about having physio on a Tuesday afternoon was that Kenny and I missed out on one science lesson of the week, which we both found boring as we couldn't do much ourselves in the science lab. Using things like Bunsen burners, making an electric circuit to light a bulb or other experiments were something we could just bloody watch Mr. Peach our science teacher do himself, and that was so exciting for some of us lads (I don't think!!). Yes, it was great to miss out on lessons at times. However, when you're having to go to physiotherapy and speech therapy every day for an hour each, which meant it cut into our education a lot, there would obviously become a point when you were behind the rest of the class and it also could be embarrassing.

Especially when it came to Maths and English, as they were two of the most important subjects in school. I never saw the point of physio, as I would rather have had more bloody education.

There were twelve physiotherapists to cover the whole school, as most children needed to have physio most days. Kenny and I had physio together three times a week. This day we were lying on the floor and Kenny had bare feet, whereas I had to have my bloody splints put on, much to Kenny's amusement, the bastard! The splints were made from very hard material which had steel rods going through it to keep them stiff.

Miss Corn then began to wrap the velcro straps tightly around each leg. I looked over to Kenny and pulled a face. He looked at me and laughed before putting two fingers up at me!!

"Sod off," I whispered, giggling.

With that Kenny's face changed to a very pissed-off look as Mrs. Shepherd, his own physiotherapist, had just walked into the room.

"Hello, Kenny, and how are you on this bright Tuesday afternoon?" asked Mrs. Shepherd in a very happy manner.

But Ken just gave her a half smile as he didn't like her, because every time Kenny had physio, Mrs. Shepherd made him do the same exercises, like trying to pull himself up into a sitting position by grasping on to a pink wooden pole.

Then she knelt over Kenny's hips and said, "Come on, Kenny. Try and do one more sit-up for me. Then I need to go and help Miss Corn walk Adam in his frame. While I'm gone, can you do some rolling up and down the room?"

The pain in my legs was excruciating. My knees especially.

Miss Corn and Mrs. Shepherd would lift me up, saying, "Okay, with a one, a two, and a three and up we go. Now hold on to the handles, Adam."

Then with Miss Corn at the front and Mrs. Shepherd at the back, both holding the walking frame, they would say, "Adam, let's try and walk slowly up and down the room. Come on now, you can do it."

I began to walk down the physiotherapy room. I said, "It hurts, Miss, no more!"

Miss Corn then replied in a harsh voice, "Oh Adam, just stop it now. You do this every day we walk with you. Right, just ten more steps, then you can sit back in your wheelchair."

As I carried on walking, Mrs. Drew passed the room. She stopped and said, "Wow, Adam, I wasn't aware how tall you were standing up. That is fantastic. Can I watch you walking a couple of steps, please?"

Mrs. Drew stood with her back against the door and with her arms folded over some brown cardboard folders. In pain, I walked four steps as Mrs. Drew said, "Well done, Adam, that was great and thank you for showing me." Then Miss Corn and Mrs. Shepherd supported me to sit back in my wheelchair.

After physio I went back over to Kenny. I knew that we'd have to ask Stephen or Gary to help us talk to each other. I wanted to ask Gary because he was the only one except for John that could understand what I was saying most of the time. However, this week John was off sick with a bug, and anyway it was whatever Kenny wanted, so I said both of their names out loud to him so he could indicate his choice.

"Stephen."

Shit. I said *Gary* a few more times hoping Ken would nod, as doing this with Stephen would take twice as long!

When we had finished tea and before we started to do our homework, which was always around 5:30 pm, Kenny and I were in the dormitory waiting for Stephen and the radio was on, as Kenny began to sing, "Ahh, ohh, ahh, ohh," as that was the only part Ken could sing.

"For fuck's sake, Ken, let Lene Lovich sing the damn song because you're shit!" I said, laughing, as Stephen walked in saying, "Bloody hell, Kenny. You're not trying to sing *Lucky Numbers*, are you?" Kenny grinned and gave a nod.

When Stephen was walking towards his bed to sit down, he said, "Well, that was a shit tea, wasn't it?"

"I liked it," I replied. I had always been a fan of mince and mash.

"Yeah, but you boys that need feeding probably don't taste the food as Harwell and Jones just shove it down your gullet," Stephen said whilst trying to sit down and laugh at the same time.

"You are gross!!" I said, smiling.

Stephen carried on, "Right, Kenny, let me get your Bliss board out of your bag."

He got himself comfortable on the bed next to Kenny so he could point at the symbols for him. "Okay, let's go. What's the first symbol, Ken?"

He ran his index finger very slowly across the top of the board. "The first word is a name. Is that right, Ken?"

Kenny nodded. Then Stephen asked, "Is it one of us lads in the dormitory?" Kenny gave a nod and a smile.

"I will say everybody's name and you can nod when I say the correct one. Is that alright?" Yes, nodded Ken.

Stephen pushed himself up on the bed with his hands as he said, "That's better. I'm comfy now. I assume it's not Ad or myself? No, I thought not. Okay, is it William, John, or Gary? Ah, Ah, you jumped at the name *John*, so *John* is the name. Correct, Kenny?" Kenny gave a big nod.

"*John* is the first word. Right, let's do the second one. Which row are you looking at Ken, the fourth or fifth? Okay, got it now, fourth row. The second word, *Kenny*. You're looking at the sixth column. They're doing words. Is it *eat*, *drink*, no? *Wash*, *brush your hair*, no? *Dress*, *undress*? Yes, you jumped at *undress*.

"Right, the fourth row again. Sensory words. Is the word *see*, *hear*, *touch*, *taste*?"

With that, Kenny gave a jump and Stephen said, "Oh no, have I passed the word?" Kenny laughed and put his eyes up in the air!

"Just shut it and tell us the next word. I've said it, haven't I? Was the word *taste*? *See*? *Touch*? Oh, you nodded at *touch*. So, we've got *touch*, *John* and *undress*, is that right, Kenny?" He shook his head.

"So, there is one more word?" Yes, Ken nodded.

With that, Mr. Jones came into the dormitory and said, "Ten minutes until homework time, and Kenny, I'll be helping you."

"Yes, Sir," I replied.

Then Stephen said, "There's one more word to get, is that right? Which row, is it row four? Okay it's row two, feeling words. Is it *hate*, *sad*, *like*, *love* or *angry*?

Kenny nodded. Stephen asked, "The four words are, *like*, *touch*, *John*, *undress*. Am I correct?"

As Kenny nodded, Stephen's face dropped whilst asking, "Can I just check which one of us you're saying that to?"

Kenny looked over at me, at which point I went white as a sheet. Was he asking about something he'd seen or heard rumours about? Fuck.

Then Stephen turned to Kenny. "I don't know what this is about. But if you two want to talk about queer stuff you need to get someone else to help. I'm not a fucking poof."

"Shut up, Stephen. I'm not a poof," I yelled.

I wanted to be like everyone else. I wanted to have a girlfriend. I'm a Catholic. But then I turned to Kenny who was looking down at the floor with tears in his eyes. At that point I thought Kenny might be trying to tell me that he was the same as John, a queer.

CHAPTER 9

"Oh fuck, why do Monday mornings have to come around so bloody quick," I thought, as Mum put a towel under my chin to give me my final cup of coffee before my school bus was about to arrive.

All the kicking, fighting, crying and screaming I've done with Mum over the years on Monday mornings hasn't got me anywhere. I still have to go, and I still despised the bloody place.

"Mum, Mum," I said, feeling crap inside. "Please can I take two of my *Top of the Pops* albums to school with me, the ones I got for my birthday?"

"Yes, Son. I'll put them in a bag for you. It's been a difficult weekend for all of us, love," replied Mum.

The bus arrived to collect me to go to school.

"Morning, Mrs. King. Hello, Adam. How are you both on this lovely day?" Mr. Stockman, the school bus driver, asked.

"Oh, we are fine. I'm going to do some gardening today."

Mum kissed me and said, "Love you, Son," before Mr. Stockman put me on the hydraulic lift. Mr. Stockman drove me away for another week at fucking school.

Whilst I was on my way I couldn't stop thinking about the weekend that had just gone. It was really disturbing me, making me very uncomfortable and sad. What happened could be possibly life-changing for all the family.

Saturday afternoon at home usually made me happy but not this weekend. Mum, Dad and I were in the lounge and Mum was just about to start cooking eggs, chips and beans. Dad was watching football.

April came into the lounge and said to Mum and Dad, "May I talk to you both, please? Adam, can you excuse us and go to your room?"

"No, why should I? And anyway, you might need my support," I replied, laughing.

April said in a whiny voice, "Oh Dad, tell him."

With a big shout and in his deep voice, Dad said, "Adam, just go to your bedroom now, and don't come out until I call you."

"Yes, Dad, I'm going."

In my bedroom, I played cowboys and indians on my bed. I loved to play that and making all the noises was fun to do. Noises like *BANG*, *TWANG*, *KERPOW* and *OUCH*. However, my cowboys and indians were lying down on the bed to have a battle because my hands kept knocking them over!

Unfortunately, there was something else that was about to explode in the lounge.

I heard my mum crying and my dad shout, "My God, April, you have your whole life to live, and your mother and I were so proud of you, but look at yourself now! You are a stupid girl, pregnant at sixteen. Don't think for one moment you're keeping it, young lady."

Then I heard a loud scream and the lounge door was slammed, and April went stomping up the stairs to her bedroom, sobbing her heart out. I tried to open the door of my bedroom. By the time I'd managed it, April was coming down the stairs with her bags packed.

Surprised, I shouted, "Shit, April, no, don't go! Stay, please, and let's talk in my room."

I saw her hesitate before walking back. "Okay, darling."

As April sat down on my bed crying, she turned to me. "I suppose you heard all that?"

"April, I think the whole of the street knows you're sodding pregnant. Dad couldn't have shouted any louder!"

We both laughed, but it didn't last long.

"April, you're not really leaving, are you?"

"Well, Adam, if I want to keep the baby I have to."

I tried to reason with her. "Oh, Mum and Dad will come round, and I will help too."

"Adam, I don't mean to be rude, but how the fuck are you going to help care for a baby? You can't do fuck all for yourself."

I started to see red. "You ungrateful bitch! I didn't get you up the duff. Maybe if you'd have kept your legs closed."

April's face went red. "What would you know about that? You're a spoiled brat. God, I've had enough of this. I'm leaving."

There was a long pause and she started to pick up her bags.

"April, you don't understand how much I need you. Please don't go. Who else will I talk to?"

She turned back, teeth clenched. "Just how fucking selfish are you, Adam? I have just told Mum and Dad I'm pregnant and all you care about is yourself and your fucking problems. For the first time in your life, not everything is about you. Yes, I love you, but you can't have everything your own bloody way."

My mum then opened the bedroom door with a concerned look on her face. I knew that she didn't like it when anyone shouted at me, even my own siblings.

"Are you all right, Son?"

I nodded, looking at Mum with her arms folded.

"Well, I'd better go now," April interrupted.

Tears started rolling down my cheeks and my face started to get hot. "April, please don't go."

She walked up our hallway towards the front door. "April, if you walk out of this house now, don't you ever expect to come back!" Mum threatened, with a wobble in her voice.

April left, slamming the door behind her. I suddenly found myself thrashing around in my chair, hitting and kicking out, crying and shouting, "Go, Mum, go get her."

Mum began to shout: "No, Son, I won't. Just stop it now or you'll get a smack." Her back straightened as she carried on. "Sometimes in life we have to learn from our mistakes. Go back and play in your room, Adam. I need to talk to your father."

Stuck in my room, I felt very alone and upset. The door to my bedroom was open and I could hear them both talking.

"Oh, Rose, life is never easy. April has now brought shame on the family. Sean kills people for a living. At least our Adam is coming on well at school, Rose, love."

"I know, and that makes me very happy, Terry." I shut my bedroom door, feeling happier.

Pulling into the forecourt at school on that cold Monday morning, I just felt so shitty and wished I knew where April was. Mr. Stockman parked up by the large ramp so he could put the lift down and get everyone off the bus.

I was being pushed into school by Mr. Jones, who said whilst pushing me towards the entrance of the school, "Did you have a good weekend, Adam?"

"Yes, Sir," I muttered.

We were always taken to see the nurse first thing on a Monday morning. Sister Grey or Sister Peters would look down our throats and feel our tonsils and I would pray that there was something wrong with me, and that way I'd be sent straight back home. But alas, that day never arrived for me!

"Good weekend?" I asked John, who was sitting next to me in our very large hall, waiting for one of my bloody pet hates of the week, assembly!

"Yeah, not bad. My dad and I went for a walk yesterday. What about you, Ad?"

"It was okay, John", I replied, with tears in my eyes.

As you are probably understanding by now, crying on a Monday morning was a ritual for me. Also I was very worried about April, where she was and how I upset her before she left. When we saw Mr. Eaton enter the school hall, it fell silent. Now, Sir was okay for a headmaster, but he was a very strict man, and you wouldn't want to be sent to his office, I can tell you!

"Good morning, children," Mr. Eaton said.

"Morning, Mr. Eaton, Sir," we answered.

He went on to say, "Right, children, let's sing our first hymn. *Morning has Broken*."

After the hymn we had to listen to a Bible reading, then we were told to close our eyes and say *The Lord's Prayer*. Trying to keep your eyes shut, say a prayer, and not move so you don't kick or hit your wheelchair when you have cerebral palsy was near ruddy impossible! I began thinking over what was said last Thursday evening, when Kenny, Stephen and I had that conversation. When John finds out we were talking about him, I'm not sure how he will take it. Especially when John becomes aware that Stephen supported Kenny to talk.

With that, Miss Ottawa, our music teacher, began to play the opening notes on the piano to the final hymn, *Lord of the Dance*.

Mr. Eaton said, "Now, children, sit up and let me hear your voices singing this wonderful hymn."

When we had finished singing, he said what he would always say at the end of every Monday assembly, "Have a good week, children. I'll see you around school."

Then we would all reply, "Yes, Mr. Eaton. Thank you, Sir."

After assembly, we all lined up in absolute silence to leave the hall without talking and went to our different classrooms.

In class, Mr. Burns, our new form teacher that year, after he took the register, said, "Right, can the children who are able take off your socks, shoes and tops, please? Then make your way to the school hall. Don't worry if you can't get your things off. Mrs. Davidson or I will come to help you."

I really missed Mrs. Drew being my form teacher. I could talk to her about anything. At least we still had Mrs. Davidson as our classroom attendant.

I was bloody freezing going down the corridor to the sports hall in just my shorts, vest, and bare feet. On my way to the school hall, John passed me as I screamed out, "John, why do we have to wear bare feet for P.E?"

Stopping in the corridor in shrieks of laughter, John said, trying to control his hysterics, "Did you just ask me why we had to wear bare feet?"

I nodded, giggling. "You're a stupid fucking sod, Adam. Now let's get to P.E before we are late."

The school hall was very large with a big stage at one end where the school put on plays throughout the year, and the Christmas pantomime, which I used to fight tooth and bloody nail to be in, because I felt without me the pantos were just shit! Now, the ceiling in the hall was another thing to be desired. How can I describe it? It was built in a concertina where it goes up and down and in and out. If we had to lie down and look up at it, we felt very strange and ill.

Our P.E teacher was Mr. Richmond, who I couldn't stand, but he was quite hot with a great arse for his age! There were six large, red mats spread around the floor of the sports hall.

Mr. Richmond said, "Right, can you all find your own mats and get out of your wheelchairs onto the floor, please?"

For the first part of the lesson, we had to roll off our mat and go to get a ball out of a basket, then try to bring the ball back to our different mats in the best way we could. But it wasn't as simple as it sounded because sometimes I dropped the ball and had to roll around the floor and get it back.

Mr. Richmond shouted, "Come on, boys. Try to be the first back to your mat."

The floor in the P.E hall was cold and hard, so the more I tried, the more my damn ball would keep rolling in the wrong direction, and I had to roll after it, and I always hit my bare elbows, shins and heels on the floor. The only one of us that was allowed some help was Kenny, the lucky shit! The next part of the lesson was working on our individual mats, trying to do sit-ups or trying to get on my hands and knees. They were both difficult tasks, and if I'm honest, sodding impossible. Mr. Richmond helped those of us who needed it, like me.

He held on tightly to my feet and ankles saying, "Adam, come on. Try and sit up, that's a good boy."

"Sir, no," I said every week, as he asked me.

Getting onto my hands and knees was easier because I was supported into the position.

Twenty seconds later, Mr. Richmond raised his voice a bit, saying, "Adam, just hold on to that position. Come on now, you can do it."

Almost crying with pain and collapsing on the mat, I said, "I'm sorry."

"Don't be sorry, Adam. Just work harder. Now let's have you back on your hands and knees only this time try to put your hands flat."

For Christ's sake, did the man not realize I had cerebral palsy! When we finished P.E, we went back to our classroom to put our uniform back on.

John then piped up, "Adam, I hope I can see you stripped again soon. I love it." With that he turned away. I smiled with excitement.

Some of the children in my class made their way to French. Kenny and I had a lesson with Mrs. Williams, our communication and technology teacher. She also taught some of the less able children more English or helped with our communication skills.

There were two other boys that joined Kenny and me in those lessons who were called Max and David, and we all shared the same disability. Both of them were full-time boarders, which reminded me of my situation, and how lucky I was not to be in their shoes.

Max would use a Bliss board and David and I had the same kind of difficulty with our speech. I was thinking, as the four of us were sitting around a large circular table waiting for class to begin, 'Bloody hell, why can't we all have the same classes all the time? It's not like I couldn't speak French or German or any other bloody language. It's just that people wouldn't understand me, however fast or slow I talk!'

"Miss, Miss, can I go to the toilet, please?" I asked, as Mrs. Williams walked in the classroom and put her books and papers on the table.

"What do you think the answer to that question is, Adam?" replied Mrs. Williams.

I said, quietly, "No, Miss."

"That's correct, Adam. You should have gone at break time. Now let's get on with the lesson. Last week we looked at animals and the sounds they make, and how we spell them. Today we are going to look at things to do with school, like pens or pencils. Why do we need them? What are they for? And finally, how to spell them? Now, can you tell me about some items around school?"

Kenny put his hand up, then Mrs. Williams supported him by pointing to his board. "That's right, Kenny. There are lots of beds in school. Can you give me the first letter of bed?"

As Kenny looked at *B*, she said, "Well done. That's right."

In that lesson, my mind wasn't on how to name things around school and spell the bloody words. I was also daydreaming about life, my problems, April, John, the past weekend and why I was asked to spell *moo* in the previous Thursday's lesson.

Mrs. Williams then shouted at me, "Concentrate, will you, Adam? Please now spell *paper* for me, and say each letter nice and clearly. But first tell me what paper is used for in school?"

I began to say, "Paper is used for writing," as Mrs. Williams interrupted.

"Stop, no, no, no. Class, can we understand what Adam just said?"

Max shook his head. "Okay, Max. I'm coming around so you can say why." Mrs. Williams then helped Max by pointing his board. "So Max, you're saying Adam was talking too fast and not taking breaths. Is that what you are trying to say, Max?"

He nodded. "Do we think Max is right, class? Because I feel he's right, Adam, and this also includes you, David. If you both speak calmly and slowly people might be able to understand you both much easier. So, Adam, can you spell *paper* for me, please, but say each letter with a big breath in between.

"Yes, Miss," saying as slowly and calmly as I could, "P-A-P-E-R," hoping that I was right.

Mrs. Williams then said, "Well done, Adam. Now try to speak that slowly and that will be fantastic."

What a cow, I hated her.

As I got older, I despised school more and more, because I felt increasingly patronised and not listened to.

That night, Mr. Jones had just undressed me on my bed, ready to have a bath. As he was about to lift and carry me into the bathroom he was called to the telephone.

He said, "I will try not to be long, Adam. Let me cover you up to keep you warm and hide your modesty."

"Yes, thank you, Sir," I replied.

While I was lying on the bed on my stomach, completely naked, something heavenly happened to me. I lay there, beginning to have some fun with myself under the sheet that was covering me up as far as my shoulders. The kind of things like touching myself and trying to have a wank was just something that hardly happened for me and most of the children, who were totally dependent on the school staff.

To my complete absolute surprise, I heard a small noise and looked around to see John there. He closed the door very quietly, which meant John and I were alone again, just like we were all that time ago at the swimming gala. The excitement built up throughout my whole body as John got out of his wheelchair and crawled over to the side of my bed and just sat on his knees looking at my bare shoulders.

After about a minute, but it felt a lot longer, of John looking at me in silence and myself getting an awesome feeling at the thought of the outcome, he said, "Slip down the sheet, Adam."

I began to lower the sheet slowly to the top of my bottom using my right foot. John then knelt up beside my bed and started to touch my back with his soft but cold hands. Then I went into a tremendous spasm as John moved himself down my bed to kneel nearer to my private parts and removed the sheet completely off to expose my naked body.

In an ecstatic but quiet voice, he whispered, "Lie on your back for me, Ad?"

"But what if someone comes in and we get into big trouble? My penis is so erect, John."

He then answered, "Well, that is more of a reason why you should turn over. We might not have this chance again. I so want to touch and see your very stiff willy and balls so I can feel and play with them. Adam, I know I see you undressing all the time, but you look beautiful when you're stripped."

I then rolled over and tried to shut my eyes as he first kissed me on the lips. John's lips tasted divine whilst we were kissing and our tongues met. John was playing with my bare nipples and that was amazing.

John then said, "Open your legs for me, Ad, please."

The more he grabbed and touched my balls and dick the more glorious and fantastic it was. But oh... my... God, as I felt the come beginning to happen in my willy, well, it took my breath away. Being touched by John was exquisite, magical and sensational, especially when I put my hand inside John's pyjama fly hole and felt his stiff cock, which was also wet. Wow, that evening was tremendous and very special for John and me.

Suddenly, there was a noise. "Go now," I said, panicking, thinking, "I just can't get caught."

"Ad, I'm going. But you know how long it takes me to get into my wheelchair. Anyway, the footsteps have passed," John said. Getting comfy in his chair and on his way out the door, he turned back and winked at me.

Mr. Jones came back from his telephone call and asked, "Why are the covers off you, Adam? You know it's not sensible for you to catch a chill." I just nodded, because I was scared.

Splashing around in the bath, I was thinking, 'If he knew what had just happened, John and I would be in so much trouble. But oh, it would be worth it!!'

On that evening after my bath, Mr. Jones lay me on my bed to dry me and put my red pyjamas on, and then helped me back into my wheelchair so I could watch the TV for half an hour.

Mr. Harwell walked with William back from the bathroom with a red-and-white striped towel wrapped around his waist.

He said, "Are you alright to walk on your own over to your bed now you're on the carpet, so I can go to get Kenny off the toilet, as he's shouting?"

"Yes, Sir, I can."

Mr. Harwell walked back into the bathroom, saying, "It's alright, Kenny, I'm coming. Did you go today?"

"Oh dear," Mr. Harwell said, as Kenny shook his head.

Mr. Jones was supporting William to dry himself whilst saying, "Okay, stand up for me, William, so I can dry your backside and then you can put on your pyjamas."

"Yes, Sir. Thank you."

Then Mr. Harwell carried Kenny back from the toilet and walked over to his bed which was next to Gary's. He asked, "Can you remember the last time Kenny had a number two, Mr. Jones?"

"No, but if you have a look in the diary and see, did he not go this evening?" enquired Mr. Jones.

"No, just a wee. I'll get the diary now."

Looking at the toilet diary, he said, "The last time Kenny went to the toilet was three days ago. Also, Adam went to the toilet last Thursday."

"Okay, Mr. Harwell, thank you. I will talk to Sister Grey tomorrow," Mr. Jones answered.

When I came back into the dormitory after watching *Please Sir*, Mr. Jones said, "Adam, I've just been told that the last time you went to the toilet was last Thursday. Is that correct?"

"No, Sir. I went to the toilet on Sunday at home," I replied.

"If you went on Sunday, then why didn't your parents write it in your school diary?"

"I don't know, Sir. They might have forgotten," I answered.

"Enough talking now, Adam, and let me put you to bed," he said angrily.

"Big bollocks," I thought. "I'm going to have to take that brown stuff tomorrow that goes through your system like a dose of salts."

Just before the dormitory lights were switched off, Mr. Jones had noticed Kenny was uncomfortable, and so he walked over to Kenny's bed. Whilst he was turning Kenny onto his tummy to settle him for the night, Mr. Jones heard Stephen whisper to Gary, "Are you aware we have three perverts in the school?"

Kenny jumped out of his skin, as Sir shouted very loudly, "Stephen, don't you ever let me hear you say that again."

"But it's true, Sir," replied Stephen.

With that, Mr. Jones said, angrily, "Do not answer me back. Tomorrow I will see you in my office and you can explain yourself."

Suddenly the dormitory went dark. Gary then whispered, "Steve, Steve what the bloody hell are you talking about?"

"Will you boys just stop talking and go to sleep now or I'll cane you all," hissed Mr. Jones.

John, who slept in the bed next to mine, asked me as quietly as possible, "Adam, who are the fucking perverts, for Christ's sake?"

I shot back, "Shut up, John," as quickly and quietly as I could.

Trying to go to sleep that night was very hard because John and I had just had great and bloody glorious sex and it was shit hot. However, I couldn't get my thoughts off Rhonda, and I had told the boys she was my girlfriend. I do like her a lot. It's the right thing to do as a Catholic. Mum and Dad love her and that's fantastic. Also, Rhonda is pretty. I do get on with her. Sleep now, Ad. Stop thinking about stuff, come on now.

John is only for a bit of fun. It's not real, for fuck's sake. You're not really a queer.

CHAPTER 10

"Mum, Dad and I went to Rhonda's house for Sunday tea at the weekend," I said to John about ten minutes before we had art with Mr. Mills.

"Did you have a good time?" John replied, smirking. "What is it like when you go to visit Rhonda?"

"Oh, it's a bloody nightmare. Rhonda and I are always sat together in the lounge in front of the TV while our parents go to the kitchen for a cup of tea and a chat. Ah, I just find the whole thing fucking shit!"

To be fair, Rhonda was beautiful, with a soft face, short black hair, piercing blue eyes, a wonderful smile, strong and smart – a bit like me. She could have been a wonderful friend if our parents didn't have other ideas for the two of us. Well, I knew my sodding parents did, which made everything a damn sight harder for Rhonda and me.

After we came home from Rhonda's, Mum and Dad were putting me into bed and suddenly Mum piped up and asked, "Do you like Rhonda, Son?"

"Yes, Mum, she's nice."

"Just nice? Wouldn't you like her to be your first girlfriend?" Mum said, grinning from ear to ear.

"Oh Mum, I haven't even thought about girls," I replied, thinking, "and I doubt if I ever will."

Dad, who was standing over my legs about to lift me into bed, joined the conversation. "I agree with your mother. You attend a very good boys school all week, which is great, but you have hardly any contact with girls, which is important at your age Adam, and Rhonda is a lovely and very pretty girl, and she's Catholic, which is important to our faith as you know, Son."

'Girls, girls, Catholic girls,' I thought, as my bedroom light was switched off. If I had my way, I would prefer to like girls as it would make everything easier. Any other bloody Catholic boy would be so delighted with what my parents have just said but oh no, not me.

I could feel the tension in the air at home between Mum and Dad this weekend. I know fucking April hadn't helped the situation by getting pregnant and leaving home, the silly cow!

Yes, I might love April, but she has really mucked everything up for me at the weekend. For a start, shopping on Saturday in Woolworths with Mum and Dad was a nightmare. Whereas April had some patience with me, they had hardly any.

Also, what didn't help matters was that the lovely girl who works behind the counter every Saturday, Tina, said, leaning on the counter, "No April today? Is she ill?"

'Oh shit.' I thought. 'Don't ask questions like that, please!' as Mum replied very quickly, "No, she's at home with a bug."

Then Mum asked, "Now, what other record do you want, Son? Come on. Hurry up please."

"Can I have number four, please, Mum?"

"*Jive Talking* by the Bee Gees. Is that what you want?"

"Yes, please, Mum."

"Okay, Son. Terry, will you go and pay, please, love, and let's get out of this ruddy shop."

Walking back to the car, Mum said to Dad in an angry and sad way, as he was pushing me, "I just don't know what to do about church on Sunday, whether to go or not, Terry. I'm so ashamed that our daughter has got herself pregnant out of wedlock."

"Well, church is a very important part of our lives, isn't it? And I am sure Adam would agree with me. Is that right, Son?"

I replied, "Yes, Dad," nodding my head but thinking, 'No, I hate bloody church.'

As Dad unlocked the car, he smiled at Mum, "We are going to church Rose, because that is what we do as a family."

Mr. Mills, arriving to take us to our art lesson, jolted me out of my memories. Mr. Mills was tall. He had shoulder-length, curly brown hair and a close-cropped beard, and like most of the teachers in school he could be strict. Mr. Mills also smoked a pipe during classes. I might have hated the smell of it, but he was one of my favourite teachers.

"You have worked very hard on making that pot. All we need to do now, Adam, is to go over and put it in the kiln."

"Yes, Sir," I replied, following him.

Obviously it was extremely hot, which meant Mr. Mills had to be ever so careful as he put his large, hairy hand over mine with a cloth around both of our hands in order to support me placing my pot in the kiln.

Then, closing the door, he said, "You can think about what colour you would like to paint your pot next lesson. Now go back to your desk and sit quietly, please."

"Mr. Mills, Sir," William said, quietly.

"Yes, William, what do you want?"

"I have run out of paint, Sir."

"What is wrong with you, William? You know where the paint is. Go and get it yourself. Come on now," Mr. Mills really shouted.

As I saw tears welling up in William's eyes, Sir said quite sternly, "What are the tears for?"

William replied, wiping his eyes, "I don't know, Sir."

"Well go and get the paint you need and carry on with your painting, please."

Poor William! He was a very lovely guy who always wore his heart on his sleeve, would never say boo to a goose, and never complained or was horrible to anyone else. So he always reacted when either he was being told off or when he could see other children in trouble. Just like myself.

Sitting back at my desk, my thoughts went to April, Rhonda and home.

Well, for a start, I missed April loads. She had always been there for me and we hadn't parted on great terms. Playing with a leftover bit of clay on my desk, my mind went back to Rhonda and just how I wanted people, especially my parents, to understand how I felt inside. But there was a part of me that was having the most difficult battle with myself and my feelings for John. If I was totally honest, I sometimes did think about Rhonda in a sexual way, just because I could feel normal and be a good Catholic like my Mum and Dad wanted me to be. I did want to please my parents and make them very happy, which was important to me but also a fucking impossible task. As I knew, being a Catholic was all well and good, but in my heart of hearts there was something different or wrong with me, which was utterly petrifying.

Suddenly Gary said, as he walked over towards my desk, smiling, "Adam, did you enjoy rolling that piece of clay around your desk, which you now have dropped onto the floor and I'm about to pick up and put in the bin for you like the good friend I am? Or do you want to keep it?"

Two of my fingers went up at Gary, just as Mr. Mills walked past me. He bellowed, "Right, boys, those of you that can tidy your desks please do so, then you can go. Except for Adam King."

"You are a bloody stupid sod!" John whispered, passing me to go out of the art room.

After I had come out of class, Gary asked, "So, did you get the ruler on the back of your hand from Mills then?"

"No," I replied. "What he actually said was I should have slapped you on the face."

"Do piss off, Ad. It's all lies," Gary answered, laughing.

Then, excitedly, John said, "Oh for God's sake, will you two shut up and let's go to Games. It's the last lesson of the day." He was obviously thinking about Mr. Richmond in his tight shorts, like I was.

We had games in the school playground whatever the bloody weather was, but on this afternoon it was quite hot.

One of Sir's favourite games to make us play was hockey, but with a damn good warm up beforehand. For those of us that were in wheelchairs, Sir would tie the hockey sticks securely around our waist and between our legs, and then he would take off the footplates and off we'd go. Kenny was always in goal with Mrs. Davidson helping him. Some weeks he would be on a mat on the floor, which made it easier for him, but we had a good time at aiming for his knees or somewhere below the waist. Ken was a great sport!

"Come on, Kenny, try to save. Look, William is about to aim the ball into the goal," Mr. Richmond called out with encouragement.

With a holler and a loud clap, Sir commended Kenny. "Wonderful save, Kenny. Good lad."

"Gary, Gary pass to me?" I shouted.

"No, no, no Gary, give the ball to me. Let us have chance of scoring at least," John bellowed, laughing.

Then I went in for a tackle with Gary, John and Stephen. "Careful, John and Adam. Remember you're playing against boys that you might knock over," Sir shouted.

As I passed John to hit the ball into the goal, John said, "If they go down, it's not our sodding fault."

"SHOT!" I screamed, as the ball left my hockey stick and shot straight past Ken's feet.

Then Mr. Richmond said to my delight, as I was sweating like a pig, "Okay, boys. That was a good game, and well done Adam on the final goal. It was brilliant."

"Thank you, Sir," I replied, feeling very chuffed.

I enjoyed playing many of the outdoor games, like football, cricket, rounders and hockey, which we played against other schools sometimes and that could be exciting. However, children with my kind of disability were never asked to play sports competitively at school. We just had to cheer them on from the side, which could be so boring as the damn school hardly ever won any of the cups or shields. Except when we played against Halford House School, and we only used to win because they were shit at everything!

Hockey was a fantastic game and I enjoyed playing it. But the best thing, and maybe the worst thing about it, was having a huge, hard, wooden stick tied between our legs, and John and I loved that feeling obviously!

While we were playing hockey, the stick would be moving and rubbing together with our willies and that was lovely, but it was also fucking embarrassing, as it meant that we would sometimes stop or slow down in the middle of the game for what seemed like no reason, because we were enjoying having a hard-on whilst trying to concentrate on the game, much to Mr. Richmond's annoyance, although he would never have said anything about it.

After the game, I felt like masturbating and I thought to myself on this warm afternoon, 'I wonder if I will be allowed to undress myself tonight.'

Then 'Oh bollocks' sprang to mind, as I remembered what blasted day it was. Once a month, we all had to have our hair cut by Jim, the school barber. He was a great guy, very jolly and always smiling.

I didn't like having my hair cut for two reasons. One, it was always cut so damn short, which I hated. And secondly, Mr. Jones or Mr. Harwell, whichever one of them was free, would assist Jim by holding my head still. I would say Mr. Harwell was gentle when he held my head but most of the time Mr. Jones would come, and he would hold my head very tight. Like it was going to fall off.

As Sir was brushing the hair off my clothes and from around my neck, I said nervously, "Sir, can I undress myself tonight for a bath?"

"I suppose it would help Mr. Harwell and I, because I am needed here to help Jim," Mr. Jones answered.

'That's fantastic,' I thought, on my way back to the dormitory.

I told Mr. Harwell what Mr. Jones had said, and he replied, "Well yes, alright, Adam. Go over to the mat and I'll help you down on to it."

Sir then undid the belt that held me in my wheelchair and lifted me slowly onto the floor. He undid my buttons and took off my callipers. He went on, saying, "But I'm warning you, Adam. I will give you an hour, so no funny stuff please."

"No, Sir," I replied.

Sitting on my knees on the dark purple foam mat, I could feel eyes staring into my back. It was John and Kenny. On turning my head to look at them with a smirk, I whispered, "Great haircut, boys! But what the fuck do you think I am, a stripper? Do you really think I'm going to let you both watch me get naked?"

Then John said, giggling, "Well, Adam, it would be very pleasing on the eye. Am I right, Ken?" Kenny nodded and laughed with pleasure.

"Oh, just fuck off you couple of perverts, and let me carry on undressing."

Just getting my grey woollen socks off took me about ten minutes. Then I put my left arm over my head to grab my grey v-neck jumper and pull it off, which was a difficult task, especially when I would bloody let go when it was halfway over my head and I had to spend the next five minutes or so trying to grab hold of it again, just to begin the process of then pulling the jumper down over my arms. My white shirt which had the buttons opened was another issue, but not quite as much of a struggle as the last garment of clothing.

Now at this point, I had bare feet and a bare top half. Lying down on the mat, I began to kick my legs and push a foot against my shin to try and lower my black trousers. This being the start of another lengthy bloody process, to try and wiggle the bastard things off.

Being in just my white y-fronts excited me very much, as I knew I was almost there.

"Look to your right, Ken. He's going to be stripped very soon. Oh, get your hand in the back of your pants and get them off, for God's sake!" John said, with excitement in his voice.

I kicked my pants off, turning myself onto my tummy to rub my body up and down on the mat, which I had to stop abruptly as Mr. Harwell came back into the dormitory and said, "Alright, Kenny, let me undress you for your bath, and John can you undress, as I'm sure Mr. Jones will be back soon to help you. Adam, I'll bathe you after Kenny."

"Yes, Sir," John and I replied, as he walked out of the dormitory with Kenny.

John was almost naked when he said in an elevated way, "Ad, I'm coming down on the mat with you, because you look so beautiful lying there undressed."

"John, I don't think that's a good idea. What if we get caught?"

"Oh, shut it and lie on your back and we can touch each other," he answered, crawling towards me.

As we had our hands on each other's cocks, my horror came true. Mr. Jones stood over us, with our hands where they should never have been. He shouted very loudly, "What the hell do you think you're both doing? Stop that this instant."

Suddenly Stephen entered the dormitory, as Mr. Jones continued shouting, "I'm sorry, Stephen, can you please go out again, close the door and wait for me to call you to come back in."

It was like my world was falling apart because I knew John and I were going to be in very, very serious trouble.

CHAPTER 11

God, the following weekend at home was difficult for me.

Mum and Dad had been called up to the school the week coming to see the headmaster, and Dad said, buttering a piece of toast after church, "I hope Mr. Eaton wants to see us about something good and not bad next Wednesday, Son?"

"Ah no, Terry. I'm sure everything will be grand. Our Adam is a good boy and he's doing so well at school. Aren't you, love?" Mum asked, preparing Sunday lunch.

I gave a nod and half a smile. I knew why they were coming to school and I was bloody petrified.

The dreaded morning arrived and I was fucking shitting myself.

"Good morning, boys. Are we ready for another nice day at school?" I heard Mr. Harwell say.

Mr. Jones came over to my bed and uncovered me. He began getting me dressed.

'Well, this is going to be a bloody nasty day,' I thought, as I was lying there and Sir put on my socks.

Then Mr. Harwell said, "John, I'm not catching what you're saying so say it again for me please?"

"I need a pair of underpants please, Sir," John replied.

"Just let me finish with Kenny and I will get you a pair from the wardrobe."

"Thank you, Sir."

When I was dressed I went over to talk to John, who was having his face and hands washed by Mr. Harwell. I hated being washed by either of them because they were so rough and if you complained about it they would really shout at you.

I was sitting on the opposite side of John's bed when he said, "So, what's with the worried look today, Ad? We only have science first lesson."

"John, how can you joke at a time like this?"

"Yes, Adam, you're right, I know. And my parents are coming up tomorrow and I'm shitting myself just the same as you," John answered, with a worried look.

Mr. Jones then said, "Right, go up to breakfast now lads please, and no talking going up the corridor."

As Stephen walked slowly past John and me, he mouthed, "You couple of queer fuckers."

I said to John, "One day I'm going to kick that arsehole's walking frame from under him. Anyway I'm not bloody queer."

"Yeah, and I will probably help you, Ad," John said, laughing as we made our way to breakfast.

"Who would like bacon and eggs for breakfast?" asked Mrs. Rainer, our school cook.

"Yes, Miss. I would love some eggs and bacon and can I have two eggs?" said Gary.

"If you can't say please to Mrs. Rainer you will not be having any breakfast," Mr. Jones said very angrily, standing behind me and holding a small towel under my chin to catch the drips when he was giving me my cup of coffee.

"Sorry, Mrs. Rainer. I mean please."

"That's alright, Gary. Adam, would you like anything?" said Mrs. Rainer.

"No, thank you, Miss. I'm not hungry."

As Mrs. Rainer walked away from our table, Mr. Jones said, "You are having something to eat, Adam, even if it's just a piece of toast and butter. Today is a big day."

Mr. Jones then buttered two slices of toast for me. But whilst he was feeding me I kept shaking my head because I felt sick and I kept on gagging with each bit that was put into my mouth.

"Come on, Adam. Just two more bites. Then you can go back down to the boarding unit and get prepared for school and the meeting," he replied.

On my way down to the boarding unit, I always passed Mr. Eaton's office and the school reception. However on this Wednesday morning as I was passing, Mum and Dad were sitting outside the headmaster's office.

"It's only 8:30 am. You're very early. The meeting is not until 9:30 am," I said, kissing my Mum.

"Yes, we know, but your father wanted to miss the traffic."

Mr. Jones walked past us holding our dirty bibs and towels, while saying in a very surprised voice as he spotted my parents, "Hello, Mr. and Mrs. King. How nice to see you again. Are you both keeping well? You're a bit early. Can I get you a tea or coffee?"

"That's just what Adam said," Dad replied, laughing as he went on to say, "Yes, please, Mr. Jones. Two cups of tea without sugar would go down a treat."

"Not a problem. I just need to get the boys ready for school. I'll tell you what. Why don't you come down to the unit and we can chat before the meeting begins? Adam, go to the dormitory so Mr. Harwell can put you on the toilet and brush your hair and teeth, and tell him I'll be along in a minute."

"Yes, Sir."

As I drove away in my new electric wheelchair, I heard Mum saying to Mr. Jones as they walked slowly behind me, "We are very pleased that we were able to have this meeting today."

Sir replied, "No problem at all. There are a few things we'd like to discuss with you both too."

Now toilets should be something that are private but oh no, not at my school. The toilet doors were just like stable doors so the school carers could look over the top of the door and ask if we could cough to open our bowels if we had been! But the worst part was the cleaners would come and start to clean the toilets, sinks and baths while we were trying to go. This got more embarrassing as I got older. Talking to a lady when you're sitting on the lavatory can stop all your bodily functions.

As I was sitting on the toilet I thought, 'The worst thing about this meeting is knowing my Mum and Dad are in school and there's fuck all I can do about it. Oh, poo!'

Talking of poo, Mr. Harwell looked over the half toilet door as he enquired, "Well, Adam?"

"Yes, Sir, I've been," which was a bloody relief and got me out of taking this horrible medicine that they would otherwise force you to have to "move things along."

After Mr. Harwell had brushed my hair and teeth and put my tie on, he said to Gary and Stephen, "Have you washed your hands and face, boys?"

"Yes, Sir."

"Okay, go up to school and I'll see you this afternoon. Oh Stephen, Kenny has gone off to school without his board. Can you please take it to him?"

"Yes, Sir, I will," putting the board into his school bag, which he always hung over his walking frame.

Then Mr. Jones said, "Adam, it's 9:20, so you can go and wait with your parents in the playroom. I'll go up to school and let them know you will be late."

"Yes, but I need to go to the medical room to have my tablets, Sir."

Mr. Jones shouted, "Well, Adam, what do you think the most sensible thing to do is in this situation?"

I replied quietly, "Go up to Sister and then come back to the boarding unit, Sir?"

Mr. Harwell was making the beds, when Mr. Jones said harshly, "No, don't be stupid, boy."

Feeling very embarrassed as my Mum and Dad were just outside the dormitory when I was being told off, I asked, "Shall I take my parents up to reception with me, Sir?"

"Yes, Adam. Next time just think. Now get out of my sight. I'll see you outside Mr. Eaton's office."

"Yes, Sir," I replied, leaving the dormitory.

Mum, Dad and I were on our way to the medical room when Dad enquired in a cross voice, "Why were you being shouted at by Mr. Jones, Son?"

"I don't know, Dad. Has April been in touch?" I mumbled.

Mum replied, "We're not here to talk about her. It's you we have come to talk about and find out about your behaviour."

"I haven't done anything wrong Mum, honest. Mum, Dad, would you like to go and sit in reception while I go to the medical room to have my tablets?"

"Okay, Son. See you in a minute," answered Mum.

In Mr. Eaton's office I was shaking like a leaf. I was thinking to myself, "Shit, I know what this meeting is about but I will deny everything."

My mum and dad were next to one another on two black leather chairs. Before sitting down next to Mr. Jones, Mr. Harwell offered the teas and coffees and I sat in front of Mr. Eaton, who was sitting in a very large, red leather chair behind his desk.

"Thank you very much for seeing us today, Mr. Eaton," Dad said.

"Not a problem. It's good to see you both. The reason why I called you both into school is that Adam's behaviour has started to become a problem over the past few weeks or so."

"Like what?" Mum asked, shocked.

"Well, Mr. and Mrs. King, he has been using bad language in school and his schoolwork hasn't been up to standard of late. Also I've had reports from Mr. Burns, Adam's form teacher, that he's not concentrating in class. And I'm afraid to tell you that Adam was found with another boy on the mat in the dormitory before his bath time."

In complete shock, Dad responded, "I don't understand. This is all very upsetting and worrying, Mr. Eaton. As for the other boy, couldn't it be that they were probably just play fighting to kill time before their bath. Am I right, Son?"

I nodded my head vigorously as Mr. Jones said, "No, Mr. King. I am sorry to report that Adam was caught touching another boy inappropriately."

Then Dad asked very abruptly and angrily, "Adam, why? What is wrong with you and why are you behaving this way?"

"Nothing, Dad!" I replied, very sheepishly.

Mum raised her voice. "Son, look at me now, and tell your Dad and I the truth. Did you do what Mr. Jones said?"

"No, Mum, honestly I wouldn't do that. The other boy made me."

I was sent to wait outside the office while my parents and Mr. Jones talked with Mr. Eaton. Shaking with nerves and feeling sick, it was around ten minutes or so before I was called back in. Mr. Eaton then said, "Alright, Adam, we have all talked this through and decided that we will draw a line under this, but I don't ever want to hear of behaviour like this again. You are going to be closely watched from now on. Do you understand me?"

"Yes, Sir," I answered, thinking, 'I am happy that's over,' but little did I know what was about to hit me next.

Mr. Eaton then asked, "I am aware, Mr. and Mrs. King, that you have a problem to discuss with us. Am I correct?"

I thought, "A problem, problem, what sodding problem?"

Dad sat up in his chair. "Yes, Mr. Eaton, and I know Adam isn't going to like what I'm about to say."

"Please just carry on with what you would like to talk about, Mr. King."

"What it is, I spoke with Mr. Jones last night on the telephone about the possibility of Adam becoming a full-time boarder, and I know he will find all this very upsetting."

I was getting very agitated. "Calm down now, Adam. Let your Father speak and you can talk after. Do go on, please, Mr. King."

"Well, there have been difficulties at home with our daughter, which meant her leaving home. This now means my wife has to care for Adam alone, and I work on Saturdays, and she just can't cope with him."

Mr. Jones looked over at me and said, "Stop the tears now, Adam. You're a big boy."

"Mum, Mum, please no. I'll be a good boy and I will help you, I promise. Just don't make me stay at school full-time, please."

Mum, wiping my eyes, said, "Listen to me, Adam. Your Father and I both love you very much, but you need to understand I can't cope with you on my own. I am sorry, Son."

Mr. Eaton answered, "Adam, we all know just how difficult this is for you, but it's a decision for your parents to make."

"Yes, Mr. Eaton. Sorry, Sir," I said, ever so quietly as I wished this was all a very bad dream.

Then the dream became a bloody nightmare as Mr. Jones said, "Last night after I'd put the boys to bed, I saw Mr. Asmara. He's in charge of the boys that board full-time and he told me they have a bed free in Mr. George's dormitory. If you would like to go and look at it and have a chat with Mr. Asmara and Mr. George?"

"Would it be possible for Adam to begin full-time boarding from next week please?"

"Yes, Mrs. King."

Mr. Jones asked, "Could I just use your phone please, to ring down to the boarding unit and see if Mr. Asmara and Mr. George are free to come up to have a talk with Mr. and Mrs. King?"

"Yes, that's fine, Mr. Jones," Mr. Eaton replied.

Mr. Asmara and Mr. George acknowledged me as they came in, both saying, "Good morning, Adam."

"Good morning, Sir," I answered quietly back.

Mr. Asmara was a very large man with dark skin and a bushy black beard, and his manner frightened me somewhat because he was harsh. Mr. George had short, brown, spiky hair. He was thin, tall, and I was aware that he was friendly and quite fair.

Mr. Eaton said to Mr. Asmara, "Mr. and Mrs. King would like Adam to be a full-time boarder from now on. Is that possible, Mr. Asmara?"

He replied, "Yes, I can't see a problem. Mr. Jones and I spoke last night about our spare bed and I also discussed it with Mr. George on the way here. We both felt it might be beneficial for Adam if he stays in Mr. Jones's and Mr. Harwell's dormitory during the week so he can still be with his friends. Then Adam can come over to us on a Friday evening after school."

"That all sounds good to me. What about you, Mr. and Mrs. King?" inquired Mr. Eaton.

Mum said, "Well, I'm happy with that arrangement."

Mr. Asmara went on to say, "I'll just need you to fill out some forms, please.

Mr. Eaton carried on, saying, "We all think that some sessions with the school psychologist, Mrs. Trotter, may help you. What do you think about this, do you think it may help, Adam?"

Holding my Mum's hand, I replied, "Yes, Sir."

"That's the right attitude to have, Adam. Well done. I hope the session will begin in the next two weeks or so."

I asked if my parents could come to see me at the weekend. Mr. Asmara said, "Yes, Adam, your parents can come to see you on Sunday afternoons between 2 and 4:30 pm. Have you finished filling in the forms, Mr. King?"

"Yes, but I've just a couple of questions. Do we need to provide clothes for Adam? Also, can we phone him sometimes?" asked Dad, standing up to put his coat and flat cap on.

I felt very, very trapped as Mr. Jones said, "Well firstly, it's much easier if the children wear their school uniform at the school. Therefore I will give Mr. George some of Adam's clothes for him to wear. Also, you can telephone Adam any time just as long as he's not in school or doing his homework. Oh yes, just one more thing before you go. We allow the children £5 pocket money a month. If you could give that to either Mr. George or Mr. Asmara that would be great," said Mr. Jones.

Dad answered, "That's not a problem. Thank you all for today. I know Adam's very upset but he is going to be strong for me, aren't you, Son?"

"I will try my hardest, Dad," I replied, still crying and thinking maybe if April never got fucking pregnant, I could probably go back home at the weekends.

I then kissed my Mum and Dad goodbye, saying, "I'll see you on Friday. I love you."

My Dad ruffled me on the head and Mum kissed me and said, "I love you too. See you on Friday." I watched them walk out of school, as my life had turned into a horror.

Mr. Eaton then said, "Off to class now please, Adam. Hold on a minute and let me wipe your eyes and tighten your tie."

"Thank you. Can I go, Sir?" I asked.

"Yes, Adam, you may. Remember you're a strong boy. You can do this," he replied, smiling.

On my way down the corridor, I stopped to dry my face a bit more, and I could hear Mr. Asmara and Mr. Eaton talking about me. Mr. Asmara said, "I think Adam is going to have a hard time being away from home all the time."

Mr. Eaton replied, "Yes, I think you're right, but it might do him the world of good. Also, I do feel Adam will benefit from us being tougher on him."

'What's the time?' I thought, looking up at the clock in the dining room as I went past. 10:50 am - ten more minutes of break time left.

"Adam, Ad mate. How did the meeting go?" John asked.

Replying in anger, I said, "What's another word for *bloody*, *shit*, *damn*, *fuck* and *bugger*?"

"Shit, did they ask about us touching each other?" asked John.

"No," I replied, lying, feeling guilty for blaming John as I had.

"So, it when well then?" John replied, laughing.

"Oh John, it was a fucking nightmare. Remember I told you about April getting pregnant? Well my parents can't cope with me at the weekends. That's right, you have guessed it. I have to stay at fucking school full-time."

I took a deep breath and carried on, saying, "John, I hope your meeting goes better than mine tomorrow. At least I wasn't caned today."

"Yes, Adam, that does make me happy, because you're the one that gets caned the most out of all of us!"

"John, fuck off! Now that's the bell, home economics is calling. Don't burn yourself this week like a dick!"

John and I made our way to the cookery class, and he was a couple of inches in front of me as he asked, slightly worried, "So does that mean you will have to move over to the full- time boarding unit? Don't leave me with them boys, Ad, please."

We were approaching the door of the cookery class.

I said, "No, I'll still be able to stay with you lovely lot in the week and go over to Mr. George's dormitory on a Friday evening after school. Now let's go and try to make some nice jam tarts with a mug of tea with Mrs. Wright. I hate this crappy lesson."

Mrs. Wright was a rotund lady with a big booming voice and always spoke excitedly. That was one of the reasons I never liked the lesson, because she talked so damn quickly. She was another person I couldn't understand at school!

The cookery class was shaped like an L, with four low ovens so we could reach them ourselves. Not that we were ever allowed to. We always had help from Mrs. Wright or Mrs. Davidson. The classroom always smelt of fresh cooking even before the lesson had started.

"Okay, boys, we are making jam tarts today. I will work with Stephen, Kenny and Adam. Mrs. Davidson, can you please work with Gary, John and William?" Mrs. Wright said.

Sitting John at the table properly, Mrs. Davidson replied, "Not a problem."

Then Mrs. Wright stood at our large, square table and said, "What do you think we need on this table to begin making the jam tarts?"

"A mixing bowl and a large spoon, Miss?" Stephen said.

"Yes, Stephen, good boy. You know where they are. Can you go to get them please?"

"Yes, Miss. I will."

That morning, I felt very, very troubled as I sat there being taught how to make fucking jam tarts just because I had to. My whole body was shaking inside with frustration, annoyance and resentment. When Stephen came back to the table with the bowl and spoon and sat down again, Mrs. Wright asked me, "Adam, what do we need to do now?"

"Make the bloody things. I don't know," I said.

Stephen, who was sitting next to me, hit me over the head with the spoon and said, "Come on, dumb head, just answer Miss!"

In my anger, with my left hand, I smacked Stephen in the mouth, making his teeth bleed. Also, with my right hand, but not on purpose, I knocked a box of eggs and a bag of flour off the table and on to the classroom floor, which made one hell of a mess.

Stephen said angrily, with blood coming out of his mouth and whilst Mrs. Davidson was holding tissues to try and stop it, "What the heck did you punch me for? You moron."

"If you don't shut it, you'll find yourself getting another one, only this time bloody harder," I retaliated.

"Come on, Ad mate, calm down, and we can talk after class," John said, being friendly.

"Oh piss off, John, what would you bloody know? This is all your fucking fault, you pervert, and I hate you," I screamed at him.

Mrs. Wright shouted, "Enough now, Adam King. I can't believe your behaviour today, and the lesson has been really spoilt because of you." As she went on to say, pointing at the floor and table, "You can also help me tidy this mess that you have made."

"Whatever, Miss. I just don't give a FUCK!!"

I suddenly saw William beginning to cry, and I shouted, "Oh for fuck sakes, William, you're such a bloody baby."

Then Mrs. Wright, in a very angry voice, said, "Don't you ever use that language in my classroom. Now get out and wait for me to come out to see you at the end of the lesson."

Making my way towards the classroom door, I heard Stephen say under his breath, "Yeah, get away from me, you queer bastard."

I spun around in my electric wheelchair and crashed into his chair that he was sitting on, and then I thumped him in the back. With that, he turned around and hit me in the face. I then kicked him in the side of his leg which unbalanced him, and Stephen fell off his chair onto the floor.

Mrs. Wright stood very tall with her hands on her hips and said loudly, "Mrs. Davidson, can you go to get Mr. Eaton for me, please? Both of you stop fighting this instant."

But I just wanted to hurt someone like I was hurting inside, so I kicked Stephen one more time in the top of his leg. "Ouch, you bloody arsehole," he shouted.

Then the class went silent as we heard a booming voice saying, "What's going on in this classroom? How dare you behave like this in school. Stephen, get up off that floor now and go to wait outside my office. Mrs. Davidson, could you please take Adam to my office too, as he can't be trusted and I don't want any more fights. Get out of my sight. I'm so cross with the two of you."

Leaving Mrs. Wright's classroom, I heard her say, "I can't believe what just happened. Adam is usually a very nice boy, and so is Stephen."

"I'll explain at some other time, Mrs. Wright, but I should go and sort out the boys now," Mr. Eaton answered.

"Okay, thank you very much for your help, Mr. Eaton," she replied.

Going down the corridor to await my punishment in Mr. Eaton's office and being escorted by Mrs. Davidson, I felt very lost and scared. I just didn't care anymore. I loved the times that John and I spent together, but it looks like those wonderful moments were over.

When Stephen, Mrs. Davidson and I were waiting in the reception for Mr. Eaton to come along, I thought, 'Bloody hell,' as I'd only been in the same spot about one and a half hours ago. Then he walked past us, saying, "Thank you, Mrs. Davidson. I'll take it from here."

"Okay, Mr. Eaton. See you later, boys," she replied.

Standing at his office door to hold it open, Mr. Eaton said, "Right, you two get in here now. Adam, you sit over by the wall. Just let me move that black chair for you. Stephen, when I shut the door you can sit on that other black chair."

Mr. Eaton, walking around, said in an annoyed voice, "Adam and Stephen, can you explain to me why I had to leave my office to come and help Mrs. Wright to stop you two from fighting?"

Through my rage, I said, "I started the fight, Sir, because I didn't like to be called queer because I'm not."

"Stephen, why did you say that to Adam?" Mr. Eaton inquired.

"Sir, Adam just started on me."

"Do not lie to me, Stephen, please."

My heart sank when Mr. Eaton said, "I am going to give you both five strikes of the cane because you both behaved extremely badly."

I looked over at Stephen, and he looked very worried and scared as Sir got up out of his chair to go to the cupboard and take out his long bamboo cane. Then Sir said, "Stephen, put your right hand on the desk for me?"

With every single strike, Stephen tried to pull his hand away, but Mr. Eaton was holding his wrist firmly. When it was my turn, Sir said to Stephen, "You can go to lunch now."

After Stephen had left the office, Mr. Eaton gave me my five lashes of the cane on my left hand as I thought, 'Why? Why do they always cane me on my left bloody hand? That's my good hand, but most importantly it's the hand I drive my wheelchair with.'

Mr. Eaton sat back down behind his desk, and leaning forward, rested his elbows on the top and clasped his hands together.

He said, "Adam, I know what's wrong with you, but you can't go around starting fights with other boys. Also, I will not have anybody disturbing classes in school. Do you understand?"

"I'm sorry," I said, with my arms on my lap and looking down at the ivory carpet whilst kicking my black right footplate.

"Adam, look at me now."

I raised my head to look at Sir as he carried on saying, "Now, we all have things we don't want to do. But we must bite the bullet and get on with it. Yes, I know that you don't want to go to full-time boarding. But this is something that they need you to do. You must be grown-up about this."

"I know, Sir," I replied, very quietly.

"Okay, Adam, off you go and I don't want to see you in my office again for the foreseeable future," he said whilst opening the door.

In bed that night, trying to get to sleep after the very bad day that I had, I was feeling really pissed off about everything, but mostly my fight with John kept going around in my head making it hard to get to sleep.

I was drifting off into slumberland when as usual, as every sodding night early morning around 3 am, I was woken up by the sound of Stephen's sticks going across the dormitory to the loo with the help of our night nurse, Mrs. Atkinson. I never took to her as she was an abrupt lady, and she didn't have patience with us. She stood tall, slim and in her forties. I never liked that time of the morning because she would wake us to ask if we needed the toilet, which I thought was a very daft thing to do if you were asleep. God help you if you piss the bed! But that morning I did have to go so I said, "Miss, can I go to the toilet, please?"

"Hold on, Adam. Let me settle Stephen back into bed, and I'll be over to you."

"Stab the fucker with a pen." I thought, as I was waiting for her.

Mrs. Atkinson then came over and she uncovered me, took my pyjama bottoms off and then carried me into the bathroom and sat me on a toilet chair, put a strap around me, and putting me over the toilet, she said, "I will be back in five minutes to get you off."

"Yes, Miss."

When I was sitting on the loo, I wished I could escape from everything, and just go back to how life was before.

"Have you had a wee for me, Adam?" asked Mrs. Atkinson.

"Yes, I have, Miss."

CHAPTER 12

It was my last weekend at home before I had to begin full-time boarding at school, and Sean was home on leave which was great.

After Sean had done all the normal things like go to confession on Saturday morning, just to keep Mum happy, and go to church of course on Sunday after lunch, Sean said, "Adam, would you like to go for a walk across the common? It's a lovely day."

As we were walking along, I felt very low and sad, so Sean sat on a bench and he put me next to him. Leaning on the arm of the bench, he said, "Right, Adam, tell me what's on your mind?"

"Sean, firstly, it's wonderful to see you. Did Mum and Dad tell you I'm going to be a full- time boarder beginning next week? Can you try and talk them out of it, please?"

Laughing, Sean replied, "How the heck do you expect me to do that, Adam? You know why you must go."

"Well, you could give up the army and take care of me at weekends."

"Yeah, like that is going to happen. Adam, come on now. It's not as if they are putting you away for ever, and you will see them every Sunday afternoon."

"Wow, fucking wow, Sean. It's not fair."

"Shut up. We both know that there is nothing you can do about this, so just grow up for Christ's sake."

On Monday morning, saying goodbye to Mum, Dad and Sean was dreadful. I couldn't believe how damn quick the weekend had gone, and looking forward to going home on Friday night was something I had always loved. That was a thing of the past now, which hurt me.

That week dragged very slowly, and at times I wished for a miracle. However I don't know what kind – just something to get me out of this shit.

Friday morning soon came around, and the feelings that I've always had at that time of the week were now gone. "Good morning, Adam," Gary said, as he was going to the dormitory sink to have his wash.

"Morning, Gary," I replied, as I went on to say whilst I was sitting there dressed and almost ready for school, "I don't know what's good about this morning, Gary."

"I know, mate. It's going to be hard for you this weekend because it's your first time away from home," Gary answered, while putting his trousers on.

"Morning, Gary. So you got up then, Ad?" John said laughing, as Mr. Harwell pushed him out of the bathroom and over to his bed to be dressed.

"Oh, ha, ha. People think they're so comical. Don't they, Gary?"

I just finished munching on a slice of toast and marmalade, as Mr. Jones wiped my chin, and taking off my apron, said, "After you have brushed your teeth, and before you go up to school, can I see you in the office, please, Adam?"

"Yes, Sir."

Leaving the dining room, David shouted, "Looking forward to seeing you later this afternoon, Adam."

I just nodded and smiled, hearing Mr. Asmara, who was feeding David, tell him off for shouting. On my way back to the boarding unit, I thought, 'Why are all the fucking staff so strict in this school?'

In Mr. Jones's office, he sat down behind his desk and began saying, "How are you feeling about this weekend, Adam?"

"To be honest, Sir, I'm scared and it's like I am getting punished for something I didn't do," I said, trying my hardest not to cry.

"Well, Adam, I understand that, but Mr. Harwell and I are proud of you. You're much stronger than you think. Mr. George, who is a very nice person, will meet you after school today and take you to the weekend boarding unit."

I couldn't stop myself. I just cried and cried. Mr. Jones came around the desk to dry my eyes as he said, "Listen, Adam. Everything might be very, very scary now, because it's the unknown that you're going into. On Monday afternoon after school, I would like you to tell me all the best things about your weekend. Will you do that for me?" I nodded glumly.

"Now, off to school and have a good weekend."

"Thank you, Sir. And you."

On my way, Mr. Eaton passed me. "Good morning, Sir," I said.

Looking at his watch, he replied, "Morning, Adam, but why are you late for school?"

"I was talking to Mr. Jones in his office, Sir."

He said abruptly, "Why? Are you in trouble, Adam?"

"No, Sir, I'm not. Mr. Jones wanted to talk about this weekend because I begin full-time boarding tonight."

"Okay, Adam. Get to school now before you're late, and I'll see you in reading later this morning."

"Yes, Sir."

We had science first thing on a Friday with bloody Mr. Peach. He was of average height, and had thin, wavy black hair. He also had a chubby, round face.

"Morning, boys. Sorry I'm late," Mr. Peach said, as he unlocked the science lab.

'But Sir, you're always late,' I thought to myself, going into the classroom. 'If I was sodding late, I would be caned. There is no justice in this world!'

William, who was sitting beside me, whispered, "God, Ad, this lab stinks."

"I know, mate, and you thought John smelt," I said in a whisper, but just so as John could hear it.

"Ad, you're a bastard. I heard that."

"Well, you were fucking meant to John, you twat. Otherwise what's the point of insulting you if you don't hear it?"

"Listen now, boys. Today's lesson is going to be about how to make an electric circuit," Mr. Peach said, as he wrote *Electric Circuit* on the black board as if we were fucking deaf.

Then Stephen whined, "Ah no, Sir, we did that last week."

"Shut up, you stupid fucker," I responded in anger.

At that point Mr. Peach really saw red and shouted, "Adam, do not swear in my classroom! Stephen, don't you ever question my lesson again or I will cane you both. Do you both understand me?"

"Yes, Sir."

On that Friday, I couldn't give a shit. The whole class fell silent with fear as he carried on, saying angrily, "John, Gary and Kenny, you can work with Mrs. Davidson on that table, and Adam, William and Stephen, you three can work with me on this table. Can you come over here, please?"

On my way to the other table, I was thinking, 'Why do I have to work with Stephen most of the fucking time? He's just a wanker!'

"Right, Stephen, tell me the first thing we do?"

Stephen responded quietly, "Take the two copper wires, a battery, and a small lightbulb and a piece of electrical tape, Sir."

Sir then said, "Yes, Stephen, that's correct. Now can you reach over the table, and show us what to do with them please?" With that, Stephen took one of the wires and attached it to the negative terminal on the battery.

"Thank you, Stephen," Mr. Peach carried on, saying, "William, what happens now?"

"I don't know, Sir."

"Come on, William. Think now, boy."

"I know, I know," Stephen shouted, putting up his hand.

"I'm not asking you, so be quiet," Sir said very sternly.

"Sir, is it wrap the other end of the wire around the base of the lightbulb?"

"Yes, William, that's correct. Good boy. Can you also do what you just said for me?" So William physically did what he had said.

"Now, Adam, can you do the next part for us please?"

I just thought, 'Well, this is not going to happen as I don't have a bloody clue. Shit!'

"Sir, I can't flipping remember."

"Adam, come on now please. I only taught you this last week. So give me the answer?"

Ad, for Christ's sake, say something before he asks why you don't know, and you don't have a clue because last week you were fucking skiving.

"Sir, is it?" I went silent as I couldn't answer.

"Adam, I'm going to get very annoyed with you in a minute. Now do you know the answer or not?" I shook my head.

Stephen said, "Please, Sir, can I say it?"

"Why don't you tell William what to do, and he can do it for you. But give your instructions slowly."

"William, attach the other wire to the positive terminal on the battery and wrap it around the base of the lightbulb using the piece of electrical tape. Now William, make sure you have done everything, and the lightbulb lights up, demonstrating a simple electric circuit."

"That's excellent, boys. I need to check on the other table now, but you should both be proud of yourselves."

"Thank you, Sir," Stephen said, smugly.

Suddenly, "Fuck, Bollocks!!" I shouted, as my left-hand caught a sharp bit of the wire on the table. "Sir, Sir!" I said panicking, "I've sodding cut myself and look at all the blood. Sir, it's pouring out."

"Alright, calm down, Adam. Let me wrap it up with some tissue, then you can go along to the medical room. Mrs. Davidson will take you."

"Ah, why can't I go on my own? I'm not a bloody baby, Sir," I said, thinking I could take this opportunity for a crafty wank.

"Adam, what is wrong with you today? Now Mrs. Davidson, can you please take Adam. He seems to have cut his hand?"

"Yes, Mr. Peach."

When Mrs. Davidson and I were going out of the classroom, under my breath I said, "I don't need a fucking chaperone."

On my way back from the medical room with a large plaster on my index finger, I bumped into William, and I said, smiling, "Where are you off to, trying to skive off reading?"

"I bloody wish. Sister Grey wants me, because of that big caravan that's parked in the school car park."

"Sodding hell, it's not that time again is it? This fucking week just gets better and better. I hate the bloody dentist. Well good luck, mate, and give my best to Mrs. Peal."

William pushed himself away, saying, "Will do, Ad, and I'll tell Mrs. Peal that all your teeth have turned black, and you need them out!"

"Thanks, mate, love you too, and thanks for asking about my hand you uncaring shit!" I said, as I carried on down the corridor.

"Adam, we have a couple of minutes before class starts. Would you like a drink of milk?" Mrs. Davidson asked.

"Yes please, Miss."

We had Eaton for our next lesson which was reading. Mr. Eaton was very nice but bloody strict. He scared me out of my skin.

Friday mornings, Sir would arrive at class with an armful of books. I sat beside John and Gary in class. Gary whispered, "Have you seen the vampires are on the prowl?"

"Yes, poor William is their first victim. I saw him just now. Next week it's probably our turn."

"Morning, boys."

"Morning, Sir," we all answered, as Stephen went on to say, "Sir, William is at the vampires."

We all laughed. Mr. Eaton raised his voice, saying, "Alright, boys, that's enough now. Settle down, please. Mrs. Davidson, can I ask you to carry on with Kenny's *Speak and Spell*, please?"

As she came over to the desk to get the book, she said, "Kenny's getting on well with this kind of book. He's able to recognise many of the words, especially in the book *Johnny goes to the Park.*

"That's great news, Kenny. Good boy. Are you enjoying the books?" asked Mr. Eaton.

Kenny gave a smile and a nod. He also made a sound of excitement. Mr. Eaton then got up from his desk and walked over to the shelf that was behind John, Gary and me. He took down two book stands, and placing the first one in front of John, he said, "Adam, I'll be with you in a minute. Just let me get John settled with his book."

"Alright, Sir," I replied, as Gary, who was reading *The Fish and his best Friend,* turned to me and mouthed, "You lucky bastard!"

Now you think I would have been sensible and kept my gob shut, as Sir was only about five feet away.

"Thanks mate, you fucker," I tried to whisper, but me being me and with my damn speech it always comes out at normal or extra loud volume. Therefore, as I thought, 'Oh, I'm in the shit now,' I heard Mr. Eaton say, "Sorry, John, excuse me for a minute."

Then he carried on, only shouting and pointing to his desk, "Adam, go and sit at my desk. I am coming over to hear you read now."

After Mr. Eaton had finished reading *You, Me and Mary* with John, Sir came and sat at his desk, and he put my book and stand down and said, "Why were you talking in class, and more to the point, why did I hear you swear? You know what's going to happen now, Adam."

"Yes, Sir. I am going to be caned."

"Yes, that's right, in my office after the lesson. Let's put your glasses on and have a read of your new book, *My New Bike*.

Sir opened the book, and creasing the first page, he said, "Right, I'm going to put this yellow piece of card under each line like I always do, and I want you to read that line for me."

"Yes, I will try, Sir."

I began reading, "Hello my name is Joe I have a new bike for school. It's blue with a n...."

"Why have you stopped reading, Adam?" he asked. "Okay, say the sound N (nuh) ICE in your head."

"Is the word *nice*, Sir?" I answered back.

"Yes, good boy. Now read to me for a few lines more. Then you can carry on reading alone until the end of the lesson."

I went on reading, "with a nice bell and."

"Break the word up to help you like I always say to you. Now tell me the first part?" Sir asked.

"*Some*?" I replied.

"Yes, that's right. And if I put my thumb over the first half, what is that word?"

"W, W *walk*?"

"No, try again," he said.

"*Where*?" I replied, hoping that was correct, as Mr. Eaton answered, "Well done, Adam. That is very good, and now put the words together and then read on."

I replied, "SOMEWHERE... And somewhere to put my school bag, books and lunch box. I liked my new bike very much. My bike was very smart."

Then Sir said something that I was pleased about. "That was great. I need to go to hear some of the other boys read now. If you need your page turning, just ask Mrs. Davidson or myself, and I'm sure Gary would help you too. But NO talking."

Reading on, I tried my hardest to read the words correctly. "My bike goes fast along the, what's that next word, now it begins with p, say that in your head. The next letter is a, and t, and h, the last letter is s, now put the letters all together in your head again and say what sounds they make too, P A T H S. Oh yeah, I know what the word is, it's *paths*. As I ride my bike, it goes fast along the paths in the park."

I was just about to ask someone to turn my page over when Mr. Eaton said, "Alright, lads, that's the bell for break. I would like you to do some reading at home this weekend. If you just read a couple of pages that would be great."

"Sir, Sir?" Stephen bellowed, putting up his hand, "Can we take our reading books home?"

"Yes, Stephen, I did just say that you can take your books home. As long as you look after them and remember to bring them back to school on Monday."

Then Mr. Eaton went on to say quite crossly as he walked over to help me put my book away, "Boys, try to be nice to each other please, or I may have to start giving out detentions. Enjoy your weekend."

"Yes, Sir. Have a good weekend too," we all said.

Before I left the classroom, Mr. Eaton said to me, "Adam, you can take your book and the bookrest to read on your own or read to Mr. George if he has time. I'll put them in your bag. Now go and wait outside my office."

"Yes, Sir."

When Mr. Eaton had finished caning me, he said, "Adam, we have spoken to you only last week about swearing, and it's just not acceptable. Now go and think on about all I have said."

When I left Mr. Eaton's office, I headed out into the playground to get a bit of air before lunch time, and it was Friday so fish and chips would probably be on my plate, with a chocolate pudding with chocolate custard to follow, oh what joy! I was sitting there moodily, with the thoughts of food and other things and feeling the cool breeze on my cheeks, when suddenly a friendly voice spoke. I was looking around at the brown autumn leaves that were falling around me, which I found calming on a day of fear and worry. It was Gary.

"What is wrong, Ad?" he enquired.

"I've just been caned and really told off by Eaton for swearing. I hate fucking school."

"Adam, you've spent half your life being caned!" Gary replied, laughing.

"Just piss off, you pig," I said, as one more crisp brown leaf made itself comfortable on my right footplate.

"How's Rhonda?" Gary asked.

"She's fine, thanks."

Then John came around the corner.

"Careful what you say, Gary Motor Mouth is here!" I said, smiling!

"Oh do sod off, you twit."

"Shut up, you two. I have a question," Gary said, before going on to ask, "Why were you both called to Mr. Eaton's office, and why did your parents both come up to school last week?"

"Well, who's a nosey bastard then!" answered John.

"Oh come on, just tell me. I'll be your best friend for ever!"

"Okay, okay, shall I tell him, Ad?"

"Yes, John, but don't frighten him."

"What, what is going on? Come on I'm really scared now," Gary answered, almost shaking, as John said, pissing himself with laughter, "Ah, Gary mate, you're so gullible, but we love you."

"So it's nothing?"

"Yes, well nothing to do with you, that is."

"Fuck off, you couple of arseholes."

Gary walked away to lunch, while shouting back, "I hope you both choke on the bloody fish!"

After John and I had finished laughing enough to speak, I said, "John, I know that was nasty to do to poor Gary, but it was the best fun I've had in a long time."

"Yeah, Ad, you're right, but it was bloody funny. I have to say it's probably just what you needed today. I do love you, Ad."

"Please John, don't keep saying that. I would love to say it back but right now I can't because my life is a bit of a mess and you know how my parents are about all that. So for now can we just keep all this to ourselves," I quietly replied.

"Not a problem, mate. It's our secret."

On a Friday afternoon, we had music, which lasted for the rest of the day. We all loved this part of the week because it was the last lesson, yippee!

Kenny entered the school hall and made his way over towards the black grand piano so we could make a semi-circle to begin the lesson with Miss Ottawa, our music teacher. She was a very sweet lady, and she always wore long, flowery dresses with a scarf around her head to match the dress.

When Kenny was settled, she said, "Good afternoon, Kenny. How are you today?" He nodded and smiled.

"You're alright, then? That's good." Miss Ottawa went on, saying, "Gary and William, can you please help me to get the instruments out of the cupboard?"

"Yes, of course, Miss," replied William, going over to help.

In our music lessons, we had a lot of instruments: drums big and small, and cymbals, tambourines, and my favourite, the maracas. There was a large assortment of instruments. Miss Ottawa would like to open the lesson with a song, which drove me up the sodding wall.

Also, this week when I was quite mardy, Miss said, "Right, Adam, would you like to start for us please? What size drum do you want to beat?"

"Oh, Miss, do I have to? Why can't you ask one of the others?" I replied, very whingeingly.

"Because I asked you. Now pick a drum and do what you're told," Miss Ottawa answered, raising her voice.

"I would like to beat the large drum please," I said in a whisper.

Miss Ottawa sat up comfortably at the piano, and with the kettle drum on the left side of me, Miss said, "You all know how the song goes, so let me hear some loud voices please. Are you ready to beat the drum as hard as you can, Adam?"

"Yes," I said.

Then Miss Ottawa began to play the song that went something like this: "Adam, knows how to beat that drum, beat that drum, beat that drum. Adam knows how to beat that drum, beat that, beat that, beat that drum."

I would be hitting a big drum throughout the song. We would repeat the same song, only changing the name and the instrument each time we sung it. Mrs. Davidson would hold the instrument for each of us, or help children play it, like Kenny who wasn't able to hit a drum or play an instrument himself. We would also sing along with her while she played the piano, and we would pick an instrument, so we were able to play and sing together.

Looking at the minute hand on the clock as it read twelve minutes past three, we sang the last song, *Yellow Bird.* I was shaking the maracas and trying to keep in time with the tune. Then, I don't know why, but I looked over at the glass double doors that led into our school hall and out into the corridor. Standing outside the doors was Mr. George, who had brought Max along from the other dormitory. They were waiting for me to finish school. I couldn't bear not going home. The sadness becoming very oppressive.

A tear ran down my cheek when Miss Ottawa said, "Thank you, boys. You can go now, and have a nice weekend."

As I was leaving the hall to go and meet Mr. George and Max, Gary said, "Listen to me, Ad. Everything is going to be fine, mate. See you Monday."

I looked over to Gary but couldn't say anything because I was too upset, and what did he know anyway, he was about to go home.

"Hello, Adam," said Mr. George, as I met him and Max.

"Hello, Sir. You okay, Max?" I answered, trying hard not to show how I was hurting inside.

"Let's all go on down to have a look at the dormitory and get you settled in, Adam."

Max nodded enthusiastically. On our way there, we passed the main entrance to the school where there were the school buses taking children home. I saw the bus that usually takes me. I just stopped and looked at the children, who I would normally be on the same bus going home with, being put on it without me.

"Come on, Adam, please. Time is running along, and I want to talk to you before tea," Mr. George said.

"Yes, Sir. I'm sorry," I answered, feeling intrigued, not knowing what he wanted to talk to me about.

I may have felt very sad and worried, but it was also a new adventure, and if I'm honest there was a part of me that was a tiny bit excited too. The familiar smell of bleach entered my nose as I went through the doors of the weekend boarding unit. We walked down a corridor, going past about five dormitories. At the end there was a massive room with a big TV in it and a lot of toys. Mr. George took me to my dormitory just before the playroom. The dormitory wasn't very different to where I stay during the week. Mr. George showed me to my bed. It was the last one away from the door in a row of three.

Mr. Asmara came into the dormitory and said, "Good afternoon, boys. Did you all have a nice day in school? And I hope you will look after Adam on his first weekend with us."

As Mr. George took off my tie beside my bed, Mr. Asmara came over to me and said, "Adam, how are you feeling about the weekend?"

"I'm alright. Thank you for asking, Sir," I replied.

Then I heard Mr. George shout at Russell, "Don't you ever use that language again or I'll cane you."

"But Sir, Edward hit me," Russell answered.

Then Mr. George shouted, "Edward and Russell, get to my office now. Adam, I will talk to you after tea."

I just nodded my head slowly, then looking down, trying very hard not to cry, I just rubbed my hand along the red quilt on my bed thinking, 'God, why am I here?'

CHAPTER 13

"What do we do now, David?" I asked on the Saturday morning after breakfast. Just saying that to David made me realise how different my life was going to be.

"Homework for two hours, mate. I'm sorry life is so revolting at times!"

"Yeah, you can say that again. It's the bloody weekend, for Christ's sake. We do schoolwork from 9:15 until about 6 o'clock every week day and now I have to do even more."

"Ad, shut up and let's go to the dormitory and get it over with."

"Why do we have to do our homework in the dormitory? We do our homework in the playroom during the week."

With a large puff of air out of his mouth, David then said, "Adam, do I look like I would know the answer to that question? I just do what I'm told. Asmara is the one to ask about all that crap!"

I was just going to say something nasty about Mr. Asmara, like what an arsehole he is. But thank God I changed my mind. Otherwise I would have been right in it up to my neck because Mr. Asmara was standing in the doorway.

"Come along now, boys. Adam, go over by your bed and I'll help you to get on your Possum. Do you have much homework?"

"I have English and a history test to do for Monday, Sir."

"Well, I think you should begin with your history test."

"Yes, Sir, I will. Please, Sir, get the piece of paper with the questions on it out of my bag and put it on the book stand for me?"

"No problem, Adam."

As he took the paper out of my bag and placed it on the stand, Sir went on to say, "I see you have a reading book in your bag. You can read to me later or tonight before bedtime."

"Yes, Sir."

I sat at my Possum with my foot on the switch, listening to the typewriter keys hitting the paper very slowly one by one. The first question was: "Who was the prime minister of Great Britain when World War Two broke out?" Of course I knew the answer, it was Chamberlain, but the other five questions were a little tricky for me.

For the third question I wrote, "Guns and bombs." I had to ask Russell the second question.

Just as Russell was about to give me the bloody correct answer, Mr. George, who was supporting Max to do his homework, raised his voice saying, "Why can I hear talking? Silence now and get on with your work."

"Bollocks! Now what do I do? I just know about two questions on the damn paper."

As I was trying to answer and typing out this fucking shit, all I had on my mind was, 'I should be in fucking Woolworths with April buying records.'

"Boys, listen, please. Who would like to go out to the park and have an ice cream this afternoon?" Mr. George asked us as we were finishing our homework. "Can I have a show of hands, please?"

Max must have looked up, as Sir said, "Max, that's a yes from you, and Adam, Russell, yes. David, Sam and Edward, no. Okay, we will leave about 1:30 after lunch. Make sure you're here on time, please, lads."

"Russell, Russ," I said, as quietly as possible. "Do I have to pay for my ice cream?"

Russell answered smugly, "Yes, unless you're thinking about nicking it, and I think the school might frown on robbery. And aren't you in enough mess without the possibility of going to jail?"

"Oh, very funny, you twat," I replied, smiling.

"It comes out of your pocket money. You didn't think Sir was going to buy the ice cream for you?"

On my way back to the dormitory after lunch to get ready to go out to the park, which I was quite happy about as it would get me out of bloody school for a couple of hours, I overheard a conversation between Russell and Sam which frightened me very much.

I heard Russell ask Sam, "Why aren't you coming to the park with us? You always do."

I was sad as I listened to the answer. "Russell, it's bad enough having to share a dormitory with him now. I don't want to be in his presence if I can."

"Are you talking about Ad?" Russell enquired.

Sam nodded and said, "You need to talk to Stephen Smith, Russ."

Russ replied, "Stephen Smith talks a lot of shit most of the school year. So why would I believe anything that leaves that boy's mouth? I only talk to him if I need to know crap!"

Then Sam said quite angrily, "Talk to Stephen and support your friends."

Russell laughed and said, "Is talking shit catching?"

Mr. Asmara came over to me and said, "Go and get your coat, Adam, and I'll help you put it on."

"Yes, Sir," I replied, but not really wanting to go into the dormitory because of what I just heard.

At the park I had a chocolate and walnut ice cream on a nice but chilly Saturday afternoon. It was a short break from my thoughts. When I had finished my ice cream, Russell asked me, "So, girls, Ad?"

"Yeah and? What about them? I have a girlfriend called Rhonda, but I'm not going to see her much now I am stuck in this bloody place," I replied defensively.

Sitting there taking in the fresh air, I went on, saying, "Do you like girls, Russ?"

"Yes, I love girls, and Mrs. Drew is gorgeous."

"Russell, she is twice your age, mate!"

"Yes, but I can look, Ad."

Laughing, I said, "This might be the reason I'm here, because you need help. Also, Mrs. Drew? What's wrong with you?"

'Russell had an amazing bum!' I thought. Growing up into a teenager looking at boys and teachers, bottoms were my thing.

"Back on the bus, lads. Adam, can I have you first, please?" said Mr. George.

"Yes, Sir, I'm coming."

Travelling back to school, Mr. George, who was driving the bus, said, "I hope you all had a good time, boys, and enjoyed your ice creams.

"Yes, thank you, Sir," we all said in unison.

That evening as we watched *It's a Knockout* in the playroom, I really missed home and my mum's egg and chips. I normally love watching *It's a Knockout*. Seeing people slipping over with large buckets of water and getting soaking wet I found hilarious. Today, however, didn't feel the same.,

I was just about to watch the final race when Mr. George said "Adam, get into the dormitory and begin to undress please."

"Oh Sir, can I watch the last five minutes of this, please?"

But as the words were coming out of my mouth, I knew it was the wrong thing to say. The other children in the playroom looked petrified.

A very angry Mr. George started shouting, "Adam King, did you just answer me back?"

Feeling very scared, I tried to reply, "No, I, Sir, Sir, yes, I no, but, but I, fuck."

The sweat was running down my forehead, as I heard Edward say to David unhelpfully, "Did Ad just swear?"

"Yes, and watch the sparks fly now!" David answered, laughing.

"Right, get into the dormitory right now," Mr. George said very, very crossly.

I felt a right stupid prat as I made my way into the dormitory with an annoyed Mr. George behind me. "Over there and begin to get yourself undressed while I get Mr. Asmara."

'Damn,' I thought, 'am I really that thick?'

Mr. Asmara came into the dormitory in a rage and walked over to my bed where I was sitting without my shirt on. He took me into the bathroom and carried on undressing me, saying, "I'm so angry at you, Adam. How dare you swear at Mr. George?"

"But I didn't swear at him, Sir," I replied, sitting there naked and wondering what my punishment would be.

"Adam, are you calling Mr. George a liar?"

"No I'm not, Sir."

"Then what happened, Adam. Tell me, please?" Mr. Asmara asked abruptly whilst he was drying me. But I just didn't know what to say, and I thought to myself, 'I'm going to be caned in a minute.'

Sir said, "I'm not going to put your slippers or dressing gown on as you're going straight to bed."

"Yes, Sir, I am sorry."

"Well, you need to apologise to Mr. George. However, you can do that in the morning," Sir replied, putting me into bed. I caught a glimpse of the clock on the dormitory wall just as Mr. Asmara was laying me down. The time was only 6:30 on a Saturday evening and I was bloody tucked up in bed.

"Adam, no talking to the other children when they come into bed or I will cane you. Do you understand?" Mr. Asmara said.

"Yes, Sir."

But I wanted to get back up and watch television with the other boys. Shortly after Mr. George brought Sam into the dormitory to have his bath, I was lying there, trying my hardest to keep very still and looking towards the grey end wall so that nobody could see I was awake.

Mr. George said, "So, you didn't feel like coming out today, Sam?"

"No, Sir. I wanted to watch Chelsea play Manchester United on TV," Sam answered.

"Bring your towel and pyjamas with you into the bathroom please. So who won the match?"

Sam picked up his towel and pyjamas, and on his way to the bathroom, he replied, "Oh, it was really disappointing, Sir. The score was four - one to Chelsea."

"Never mind, Sam. Better luck next time. Okay, can you sit on the toilet for me, please, and try to go?"

"Yes, Sir, I'll try, but I did have a number two yesterday."

After his bath Sam came back into the dormitory. He walked over towards my bed whispering very quietly as he didn't want Mr. George to hear.

"What are you doing in bed, you bloody poof? Are you going to answer me, or I could come over there and you can put your hands down my pyjama bottoms and feel my dick? Come on, Adam, you will enjoy it, because you're sick like that."

"Oh, just piss off. Go and annoy someone else. Anyway I'm not allowed to talk to you, which is a good thing as you're a twat," I said.

It was at times like these I really struggled with being gay. However, I wanted to be who I was, even if it did mean Mum, Dad and some of the boys at school rejecting me.

On Sunday morning I was being fed my breakfast by Mr. Asmara. I knew I was still in trouble after last night.

I said, very worried, "Sir, Sir."

"Yes, Adam, what do you want?" Mr. Asmara replied very abruptly, as he scraped my last morsels of Weetabix from my breakfast bowl and put it into my mouth.

When I had finished my mouthful, I said ever so nervously, "Please, Sir, can I?"

"Yes, Adam, can you what?"

"Please, Sir, can, can, can I?"

By this time everybody had left the dining room. "Adam, go back to my office and I'll talk to you there, and you also need to apologise to Mr. George for last night."

With that Mr. George walked back into the dining room to pick up the dirty bibs that he had forgotten. As he picked them up, Mr. Asmara said, "Now we are alone, Adam, you could apologise to Mr. George here."

Sir pulled out a chair and sat down in front of me. Mr. Asmara stood behind him. I felt anxious as they waited for me to start talking.

"Come on, Adam please. We haven't got all day," Mr. Asmara said, very angrily.

"I am very sorry, Sir," I said.

Mr. Asmara went on to say, "Tell Mr. George what you're sorry for, please."

"I'm sorry, Sir, for swearing."

"Well, thank you for apologising to me, but Adam, I do not want to ever hear you swear again. Do you understand me?" Mr. George said.

"Yes, Sir. I do."

"Now go down to the boarding unit and I'll be with you in a few minutes to clean your teeth," Mr. Asmara said.

Except for going to church, Sundays at home were grand, with Mum cooking her wonderful roast. Mum's potatoes are to die for!

"David, David," I said excitedly, while we were on our way to the school sports hall to play skittles with Mr. Richmond, the P.E teacher. "David, what's the date today, is it the 18th?"

"No, it's the 17th today, Ad. Why do you ask?" enquired David, as we were all instructed to line up at the other end of the hall, so we could try and knock down the skittles that were lined up at the far end.

"I asked you the date because..."

"Right, who would like to go first?" asked Mr. Richmond.

Max jumped. "Okay, Max, shall I help you throw the balls?"

Max nodded and smiled, took his turn, and knocked over eight skittles. David and I were talking quietly at the other end of the row. He whispered to me, "Will you bloody tell me what is so important about today's date?"

"Yes, but you can't ever tell anyone else. Do you promise?"

"Yes, I promise. Cross my heart, well I would if I could!"

"Adam, it's your go now," said Mr. Richmond.

"Sir, do I have to play?"

"Yes, you do, and it will give your arms some exercise."

I chucked the ball with the help of Mr. Richmond. However, with the throw of three balls I just knocked down five skittles which was shit.

"I asked the date because it's the due date of April's baby tomorrow if it's the 18th," I said.

Then David asked in a very shocked manner, "Baby? You? April? Expected tomorrow? Oh, God please don't tell me it's."

"David, please, please don't ever finish that sentence, I beg you!" I replied with a smile but feeling sick.

"So who's April then? Also why is she pregnant?" David asked.

"Well, you better sit down for this. Oh sorry, you're sitting down already!" I said, giggling.

"You're such a child. Just fucking tell me."

I was just about to when Mr. George came into the sports hall and said, "Boys, come on please or you will miss lunch."

"Yes, Sir, we are just coming now," I answered.

On our way to the lunch hall, David said, "Will you tell me more after lunch, Ad?"

"Yeah, oh, just one thing to keep you thinking whilst you eat. April's my sister. Don't swear. We are just about to go in to eat, and they're already saying grace."

God, school roasts were always dry, and their semolina was just like glue. Sunday afternoons were recreational, and a time when our parents and family were able to come and visit us for a couple of hours.

"Alright, would anybody like to play a game with me?"

"Ad, I'll play draughts with you, but please note I am brilliant," Russell shouted across the playroom.

"Okay, just don't cry when I win, because I am fantastic."

"Oi, Adam!" David bellowed, while Russell was setting up the draughts board for us to begin our game. "You, get in the dormitory now."

"Well, well, well this is interesting. When did David become in charge and more to the point, what have you done?!" Russell asked, with a smirk.

"Coming now. Please don't cane me, David!!" I said, on my way over to the dormitory.

When I got there, David said, "Just finish what you were telling me before lunch, Ad."

"My sister April is having a baby sometime soon, so that's why I asked you the date."

"I didn't know you had a sister?"

"Yep, I've got one sister and one brother. Can I go and play draughts now?"

"No, no, tell me more. Why is the baby such a secret?"

"Well, David, I come from a very strict Catholic Irish family and April got pregnant at sixteen. As a Catholic, you shouldn't have sex before marriage. If my Mum and Dad knew I'd told you, they would probably throttle me. Bloody hell, David, all you have to do now is shine a bright light in my eyes and it would be like an inquisition!!"

"Oh, I'm sorry, Ad, I am just nosey."

"Well yeah, you are, but now you bloody know."

Suddenly Russell came to the door of the dormitory and said, "Are you coming to play this bloody game of draughts or is David keeping you in detention?"

"Alright, I'm coming now. Wow, I've never been in so much demand. I feel like Superman!"

"Oh, just shut your gob and let's play the fucking game."

"So what did David want you for?" Russell asked, as we made our way over to the table to begin our game.

"Oh, he just wanted my advice about girls and sex!"

"Yeah, right! You start, Ad. I'm polite like that," said Russell.

After several moves I asked, "Can you move the black draught on the fifth line and over the two white ones, please?"

"Bloody hell, that's a really good move. If I do that, you'll be winning," Russell answered, begrudgingly moving the piece for me.

"Move the draught and take what's coming to you," I smiled.

Russell suddenly looked up and said, "Is that your Mum and Dad over there talking to Mr. George?"

"Yes, it is. How did you know that?"

"It's a gift."

"Yeah, whatever. I will thrash you again at draughts another time, Russ."

"Hello, Son," my dad said, as he stood at the table where Russell and I were playing. "I'm sorry but I don't know your name."

"This is Russell, Dad."

"Are you having a good game, and who's winning?"

"Adam is winning, Sir," Russell replied very shyly.

"Adam always beats me at games at home, Russell. Would you like me to take him away for a while?" Dad said, laughing.

Russell nodded and smiled. With a smile on my face, I said, "This is not over, Russ."

"Oh leave the poor boy alone, and come to say hello to your mother, and we can go for a chat in the dormitory. See you later, Russell. It was very nice to meet you."

When Dad, Mum and I went into the dormitory, David and his mum and dad were sitting by his bed. Dad smiled and said, "Hello," as we walked past them to get to my bed. Mum kissed me and sat on my bed. Mum and Dad took their coats off.

Dad said very harshly, "I don't like what I've been hearing about your behaviour this weekend from Mr. George, Son. Well, what do you have to say for yourself, Adam?"

"I don't know why I swore, Dad. It just came out," I replied worriedly, as I knew how my parents feel about swearing.

Mum then said, "Your Father and I don't ever want to hear reports from school like that again, do you hear me?"

"Yes, I'm sorry, Mum. Mum, Mum, please can I come home? I don't like it here at the weekends," I asked, nearly in tears.

"Oh Adam, we have been through this. As much as we love you, I just can't look after you without help. I am sorry, Son, but it's not possible."

Then Dad said, "Adam, you haven't even given it a chance. This is just your first weekend away from home, but the other boys seem very nice and friendly."

Mum, smiling very happily, said, "I had a letter from Sean. He might be coming home on leave for his 21st birthday in a few weeks if he can get the time off."

"Wow, that's great news, Mum. I really miss him. Will you have a big party?" I asked.

"Yes, of course we will," Dad answered. "Adam, now listen to me. In about two weeks time, the Easter holidays are coming up."

"Yes, Dad," I responded very anxiously, worried about what the outcome of his next sentence would be.

"You need to be strong for us now. Mum and I have been speaking together at home. On Friday morning, I telephoned Mr. Asmara to discuss the possibility of you going into a home for the Easter holidays."

"Please no, no, no Mum! Please, I want to be at home with you, Dad and Sean."

"Oh Adam, come on. You're fourteen years old, so try to understand and stop this behaviour. It's not like your Dad or myself are abandoning you. We will come to see you as much as we can, and I'm sure Sean will come too when he's back home."

The conversation went back and forth for a little while, but nothing I said seemed to change their decision.

Looking at his watch and seeing it was 3.45 pm, nearly time to go for tea, Dad said, "Love you, Son. Now have a good week and see you next Sunday, and we'll take you out for lunch, if you are a good boy."

"Bye. I love you both. Oh and Dad," I said, as they walked out of the dormitory. "Have you given some money to Sir for me?"

Mr. George replied, "Yes, Adam, your Father gave me your pocket money when he arrived and I have put it in the safe."

"Thank you, Sir," I replied.

"How was your visit with your Mum and Dad, Adam?" Russell asked, coming through the door of the dormitory to wash his hands before tea.

"Oh Russ, it was nice to see them, but I might be going into a children's home for the Easter holidays."

"Have you washed your hands, Russell?" Mr. George said as he came into the dormitory.

"Yes Sir, I have," he said, putting his hands out for him to check.

"Well done. Now off you go to tea."

We were eating fish or meat paste sandwiches - it was impossible to tell the difference.

"Sir," I said, as Mr. Asmara was feeding me.

"Yes, Adam, what can I do for you?" he said, putting another piece of sandwich in my mouth.

As I swallowed my mouthful I said, "Sir, when do we break up for the Easter holidays?"

"Adam, you know you're not allowed to talk at the table, except for questions about eating or drinking. So I'll tell you after tea. Now just be quiet and eat," he replied very sternly.

"Sorry, Sir," I said, hoping Mum and Dad would change their minds so I would be able to go home during the Easter holidays. Oh damn, the thought of going into a children's home just filled me with dread.

I was feeling quite down when I heard someone shouting across the playroom, "Telephone call for Adam King." The telephone was just up the corridor from the playroom. When I was going up to the phone with Mr. George, he said, "Don't be long please, Adam. Five minutes at the most."

Mr. George said hello to the person on the other end of the telephone to find out who it was. My heart sang with excitement, as I thought it might be April ringing about the baby. He then held the receiver to my right ear.

"Ad, it's me, April. You're now an uncle. I had a baby boy on Friday morning weighing six pounds four ounces."

"Oh April, that's wonderful. Do you have a name yet?"

"Yes, his name is Peter Albert."

"And the surname is?"

"No, no, no, Ad. I'm not that stupid. You don't get to know who the father is that way. But I might tell you one day."

"Have you told Mum or Dad?"

"I spoke to Dad on the phone yesterday afternoon and told him."

"But I saw Mum and Dad today, and he never said a word about you or the baby."

"That's because I wanted to tell you myself. Dad told me that you were staying at school at the weekends now. I bet you hate it, Ad?"

"Yes I do, April. Did he say why Mum asked for me to go full-time boarding?"

"No, Dad never said why, but I could probably take a guess."

With that, Mr. George said, "Say goodbye now, Adam, please."

"April, I have to go now. But can you come and see me very soon?"

"Yes, I'll try and come next Sunday with Peter. Love you and miss you very much."

"Bye, April, love you too."

Mr. George put the phone down. I felt happy that I had spoken to April, but sad because I missed her a bloody lot.

CHAPTER 14

Back in my weekly dormitory, John asked, "Did you have a good Easter holiday, Gary?" as we were sitting in the dormitory after tea on our first afternoon back.

"I had a great time. We went to see my Nan in Eastbourne for a week and it was fantastic to be by the sea."

"Kenny, how was your time at home?" William asked, holding his board up for him.

Ken looked at the words as William pointed to them: *shopping, lots, Mum.*

"God, I bet that was fun, Ken," John said smiling, and Kenny shook his head laughing and putting his eyes up in the air. This was Kenny's way of showing if he was pissed off or had the bloody arsehole with someone!

"Stephen, how was yours?" asked Gary.

"Mine was fantastic. I spent most of the time with Amanda, my new girlfriend."

"How old is she?" I asked.

"Why do you want to know, Ad. Girls aren't your thing."

I was just about to say something nasty to the fucking bastard when John spotted Mr. Jones approaching the dormitory and very quickly said, "Adam, tell us about your holiday now, please."

"Thank God for John," I thought as I began to say, "My Easter was terrible. I went to a Catholic children's home for boys. I was the only boy with a disability, and nobody was able to understand my speech."

"I bet that was bloody awful for you," said William.

"Yeah, I despised every second I was there. Tim, the boy I shared a room with, was very nice."

Mr. Jones, who was in the dormitory getting the things ready for our bath, said, "Right, enough chatting now. It's time to do your homework. Kenny, I'll have you for your bath please and you can do some work with Mr. Harwell after." Kenny nodded.

My homework that Monday evening was to type about what I did in my school holidays. It was always the fucking same, every first day back after a break. I was sitting beside John thinking what to type when he said quietly, "Tim, was he, you know?"

"Oh yeah, especially when he was in the nude."

It was a difficult task trying to write something positive that day, but I just wrote about two days where I went out on trips which were great fun. One was a trip up the River Thames and the other was to Chessington Zoo. I hadn't been to either of them before, so typing about the two days was a kind of escape from one hell of a shit time.

Once we had finished our homework John asked, "Are you going to have to go to the children's home every school holiday now?" The thought had never occurred to me and I suddenly felt very worried about the summer holiday.

"I don't ruddy know. If it was my choice, I wouldn't ever fucking go back," I said. "Also, now I'm a full-time border, I get the feeling I'm not wanted at home, which makes me feel very sad because I used to love being at home with everyone."

"Would you like me to ask my Mum and Dad if you can come and stay with us in the summer holiday?"

"Thanks John, that would be bloody brilliant, but I just know my parents would never ever have that, and we both fucking understand why they wouldn't let me."

"Ad, Ad, don't get yourself upset, mate."

"I think if I could take my life, I sodding would," I said crying.

"For Christ's sake, Adam. Things can't be that bad, can they?"

"I suppose not. At least I did see April a couple of times when I was in the home. She came with Peter, my nephew."

"I bet that was lovely?" John said with a small smile.

"Yes, he's a cracker just like his uncle! Oh, and I have some exciting news too. April is going to make an honest woman of herself and marry Peter's father."

"That's fantastic, Ad. Are your parents pleased?"

"You're joking! They don't even know, because if they knew who the father was, April would be hung, drawn and quartered and the father wouldn't be far behind her!"

"So do you know who the father is?"

"Yes I do, at fucking last. It's the boy next door called Robert. He was fifteen when he got her up the duff."

"Thanks, Ad, that was one of the most enlightening conversations with you I think I've ever had!!"

"Just to finish off, I'm going to the wedding in May."

John then said, which completely surprised me, "Do you think we'll ever be a couple after we have finished school?"

"What?" I said, really shocked. "How can two men be a couple?" I carried on, "John, I have a fantastic time with you and it's been wonderful. I want to say I'd just love to be a part of your life when school's over. I just can't give you an answer now," I replied, while thinking to myself, 'How fantastic that would be, although I would have more bloody chance of walking on water, with my parents' beliefs.'

John's face fell and he looked sad as I went on talking. "With all the stuff that's going on in my life! So let's just enjoy what we're doing for now."

God, I felt like shit that Monday night going to sleep. With all that stuff floating around in my head, it was next to impossible. Also, I'd wanted to say yes to John so much because I was beginning to fall in love with him.

First lesson on a Tuesday was Drama with Mr. Edmonton. This was my favourite lesson of the week. I really liked him. He was short, with a bald, round head and he had dark skin, and we were able to have a laugh with him.

When we were all in the school hall, Mr. Edmonton said, "Good morning, boys. We are going to carry on working in the same pairs, just as we were before the Easter holidays. So get together with the person that you were with last lesson please, and find a large space in the hall."

Gary and I worked together before Easter. We found a space at the back of our large school hall. Mr. Edmonton said in a loud voice, "Right, boys. In your pairs. I would like you to keep on working with the idea that

I gave you last term please. You have thirty minutes, then you can each show your work to the class."

"Gary, I hope you can remember what we were doing last term?" I said smiling.

"Yes, I can remember what we did because I have a brain!"

"Shut up and let's get on with it. There was a bomb in a box on the bus we were travelling on. Am I right?"

"Yeah, Ad, well done."

"Gary, I might like you but you're a patronising fucker!"

"Thanks for that. Now shut your gob and let's get the bus set up. We need six chairs."

Gary and I began to get the chairs together. I dragged three of them over to our space, and started to put the bus together with my feet. "Can you remember what seat the bomb was under, Ad?" Gary asked, putting the last chair into place.

"Yeah, it was under the middle chair on the left side."

After Gary and I had a couple of run throughs and blown ourselves up in the process, Mr. Edmonton said, "Alright, lads, can you all go over by the windows and sit in a row please? Then you can watch each other's work. Gary and Adam, you can go first."

When we had finished our excellent piece, Sir asked everyone to give constructive feedback. I looked over and Stephen's hand was up.

I whispered to Gary, "Here we fucking go, the moron is about to speak!"

"Sir!"

"Yes, Stephen, what's your question?" Mr. Edmonton asked.

"It was quite good. But whereabouts was the bomb on the bus?"

"The bomb was under the middle chair of the bus on the left side," said Gary.

"Then why wasn't it clearer?" Stephen said, in a sarcastic manner.

My fists clenched and my knuckles went white as I thought, "Please answer him, Gary, before I knock the prat out!"

Gary replied with some annoyance, "Stephen, I don't mean to be rude, but we were told to give constructive feedback and I'm not sure what you said was very helpful."

He was about to give a sarcastic answer back, as only Stephen knows how, when Mr. Edmonton said to my delight, "Alright, boys, let's watch another pair. Stephen and Kenny, can you show us your work now please?"

Kenny's and Stephen's piece was good. It was about a mugging. Stephen was at a bus stop in Oxford Street. He looked around and then he said to a lady, "I love coming here to all the fantastic shops." He was just about to get on the bus when Mrs. Davidson pushed Kenny to sneak up behind Stephen and bash him over the head, then run away with his wallet.

Mr. Edmonton said, "That was great, boys. Do you have any questions, class?"

I just wanted to say, "You lucky bastard, Kenny. There are many of us who would give every bloody thing to whack Stephen over the fucking head and get away with it!"

Then Mr. Edmonton said, "Thank you for today, boys. That was a great lesson. I'll see you on Thursday."

CHAPTER 15

Schooling for me, and many of us, was pretty much the same throughout our time at Bright Side. I was desperate to leave at sixteen but alas, this was much to the disgust and annoyance of my parents, as they were insistent I stayed at school until I was eighteen.

Yes, I kind of understood that Mum and Dad only wanted the best for me, but I was having more of a struggle with school. From the age of about fourteen or fifteen I really began to despise school more and more. This was due to the similar education we were made to endure daily. Another issue for some of us was the boarding situation we had to encounter.

I recall there was a television programme that John, Gary and I desperately wanted to watch called the *Rock Follies*. It was on Wednesdays at 9 pm and that was way past our bedtime. (Yes, I still had a fucking bedtime at fifteen years of age!)

Sitting in class waiting for English, our last lesson, I turned to John and said whilst rubbing his arm, "John, my love. You're the bravest out of myself or Gary. So can you ask Mr. Jones if we could stay up late tomorrow night and watch the *Rock Follies* please?"

"Adam, I might love you very much, but do I love you enough to get the fucking cane? Not likely! Ad, you've been caned many times before so once more won't make a difference!"

"Thanks, you're a shit!" I replied, slapping John on the back hard.

Mr. Burns came through the classroom door just as John shouted, "Ouch, you fucking bastard, that hurt!"

I tried my hardest not to laugh as Sir bellowed, while slamming his books and papers onto the desk, "John, did I just hear you swear?"

"No, yes, Sir. I don't know, Sir."

I was sitting next to John thinking, with my head down, 'Bloody hell. John, just answer him honestly now, for Christ's sake!'

Standing at the table where John and I were sitting, Mr. Burns said very angrily, "The more you lie to me, John, the greater your punishment will be. So tell me the truth. Did you swear at Adam?"

I felt my jaw drop as John replied ever so sheepishly, "Yes, Sir, I did swear at Adam, and I'm sorry. But Sir, he provoked me."

Walking away to the front of the class, Mr. Burns said, "Well I am so annoyed now. I think I will give you all one strike of the cane before the end of the lesson."

My immediate thought was, 'Why do we all have to be caned? For fuck's sake, Mr. Burns is such a sadistic bastard!'

Kenny looked shit scared as soon as he knew that he was probably going to be caned, as he'd only ever had a smack on the hand.

Then Mr. Burns said loudly, "Right, boys. If I say some sentences, can you give me the word I have missed out of the sentence?"

"*I was walking down the street I saw a young man fall over.* So, class, can you tell me what the missing word is?"

William put up his hand saying, "Is the answer *when*, Sir?"

"Yes, William, good boy. Now John, give me another sentence with the word *when* in, and spell the word *when* out for me?"

'How much longer do we have to take this crap?' I was thinking, as I kicked my calliper iron bar quietly, while John answered, "Another sentence with *when* in could be, Sir: *Wednesday is the day when we go for a walk.*"

"Yes, that's right. Good boy. Now spell it?"

I always thought Stephen was stupid, but I didn't think he was thick enough to say to Mr. Burns on this day we were all about to be caned, "I know how to spell it, Sir."

"Well carry on then," Sir replied.

My heart was nearly coming out of my chest as I knew what the mad fucking git was going to say. Out of Stephen's mouth, with laughter, "Is the way to spell *it*, Sir, *I T*?"

With closed eyes I prayed, "Please, God, get me out of this mess."

Mr. Burns then shouted, "Stephen, you've wasted my time, and if you don't stop laughing now, you're all have two strikes of the cane."

My anger inside went into a rage when the whole class was lined up and given two strikes on the back of the hand. For myself and Stephen this wasn't such of a hardship as we had been caned before.

Mr. Burns said to my horror, "Kenny, I'll have you first, please."

We all followed on from Kenny. While we were being caned, Mr. Eaton knocked at the classroom door.

"Come in," said Mr. Burns, giving William his second strike.

Shockingly Mr. Eaton asked, "Mr. Burns, why are all the boys being caned?"

"For swearing and mucking about in my class, and I won't have it," Mr. Burns replied.

Sir carried on, saying, "I'm sorry, Mr. Eaton. Can I help you?"

"Yes, I need to talk to the boys about tomorrow but I'm not sure if this is the best time," answered Mr. Eaton.

"There is ten minutes until the end of the lesson. I'm quite happy for you to use that," Sir said, sitting down behind his desk.

Fuck me, what just happened? We have bloody sore hands, Kenny is in tears, and tonight I'm going to commit murder, preferably Stephen's!

Mr. Eaton went on to say, "Tomorrow morning, boys, Mr. Read, the careers officer, is coming into school to talk to each of you about what you might like to do when you leave school. I'll be asking you all to come to my office one at a time. So in the morning I will let you know what time you're needed. Thank you Mr. Burns for your time."

"Not a problem, Mr. Eaton," Mr. Burns said, standing up to dismiss the class.

After school I was going across the playroom just the same as I have done for the last six years or so. I was really pissed off on this day. I had a very painful left hand and I could hear crying coming from our dormitory, and as I went through the door, Kenny was in Mr. Jones's office with the door open and ABBA's *Dancing Queen* was playing on Capital radio. So I had to really listen hard to hear what Mr. Jones was saying to Kenny.

I first heard him say, "Now calm down, Kenny, and I'll wipe your eyes and get your Bliss board out then you can talk to me."

I sat there listening. "Right Kenny, may I take an educated guess as to why you're so upset?"

Kenny must have nodded as Sir went on. "It's because you all had the cane this afternoon?"

I presume that Mr. Jones was holding Kenny's board, as I could hear mainly single words.

"Kenny, is it the row with *feeling* words?"

I then heard five different words, which were *sad, hand, pain, frightened* and *home*.

"Kenny, listen to me. I understand you haven't been caned in school before, so you're one of the lucky ones. Just remember that and always be a good boy."

With that, in Sir's office there was a large rumpus, as Kenny made a lot of noise.

Mr. Jones shouted, "Just stop it now before I cane you myself. Do you want your board again, Kenny?"

Then Sir said four more words, and they were *not, me, boy* and *good*.

Stephen came into the dormitory to wash his hands.

"Are you okay, Adam?" he said, caressing his fingers with the soap.

I thought, 'Remember your faith, and you are disabled and gay. So adding murder to the list might be a problem.' However. Going to Borstal could be fun with all those hot amazing boys!

Gary and John came in to also wash their hands before tea as I replied to Stephen, saying, "I'm alright thanks, but if you take my advice, it might be best for you to keep your gob shut tonight. Also, don't go too near Kenny's arms!"

"Why, what's wrong with Kenny's arms?" Stephen enquired.

"What the fuck is wrong with you today? I know you're stupid most of the time but today has to be an exception, as you have made us all bloody angry. Therefore, if you go near Kenny, he's going to either give you a black eye or knock you out, and I know which one I would prefer to see."

I then heard Gary whisper to John, with a smile on his face, "God, Ad's in a right mood. I've never heard him talk to anyone like that before. For fuck sake, don't let him loose with a cane!"

"If you two don't fucking belt up, you will also get the end of my tongue!" I said, going up the corridor to tea for the umpteenth bloody time. "John," I said, sitting at the tea table waiting to say grace. "So are you going to be a brave boy, and ask Mr. Jones or Mr. Harwell if we can stay up late tomorrow night and watch the *Rock Follies*?"

"In a word, Ad, no," John replied.

"I suppose you want me to ask Sir?"

"Oh Adam, you're a fantastic friend, and Gary and I will support you all the way. Won't we Gary?"

"Of course. We'll be just outside the office when you are asking Sir," Gary said, just as Mr. Jones arrived at the table to feed us our tea, and in a stern voice he said, "Ask Sir what?"

He then sat down beside Kenny and, putting a box of tissues on the table, he asked once again with wide eyes and slower but louder, "Come on, boys. Ask Sir what?"

Beginning to shake as Mr. Harwell sat between John and myself, I said, "Sir, it's nothing, don't worry."

"Adam, I know that you're lying to me. So I'll see you in my office straight after tea."

I just glared at Gary on the other side of the table, angry thoughts spinning around my head. What the fuck did I suggest it for? You bloody knew that nobody else would have the guts to ask Sir. Now Ad, you either ask Sir for what John, Gary and you want, and it might go all right, but I doubt it. Or you lie and get the cane twice in one day. Fucking hell, what a bloody mess.

So obviously I found myself in Mr. Jones's office after tea. Sir, perching on the corner of his desk, said very sternly, "What was that all about at teatime? And if you're sensible enough, Adam, you will not lie to me."

I either lie to him, and Sir always bloody knows when we are lying.

'Oh well,' I thought, 'here goes, as I said, shitting myself, "Sir, tomorrow evening may Gary, John and I..."

"Come on, boy. What have you stopped talking for?" shouted Mr. Jones.

Taking a deep breath thinking 'Ad, you can do this,' I carried on, saying, "Can we watch the *Rock Follies,* please, Sir?"

"What time is it on, Adam?" Sir enquired.

"9 o'clock, Sir," I replied, thinking, 'I just know that we are not going to be allowed.'

Sir then stood up and walked behind his desk, chewing the top of a pen. Which meant there was about two minutes silence, but it felt like forever.

Suddenly I nearly jumped out of my fucking skin, as Mr. Jones said loudly, "I think you need to go and do your homework because I need to talk to Mr. Harwell about this."

"Yes, Sir," I replied, hoping that the answer would be yes, but in my head, I was saying, 'Be realistic, Ad. Those bastards are never going to bloody let us stay up for just one hour!'

When I came out of Mr. Jones's office, I went over to my Possum to begin my homework, and putting my foot into my switch, John asked, "Well, Ad?"

"Well fucking what, John? Did I get my arse kicked for you and Gary? No, I bloody never," I replied with steam coming out of my ears.

"Adam, we are sorry, mate. Aren't we, Gary?" John answered.

"Just bloody fuck off and let me do my homework. I'm totally pissed off with the lot of you today."

The next morning after breakfast, Gary, John and I were called into Mr. Jones's office. As we all lined up in front of Sir's desk, he said, "Well boys, last night Mr. Harwell and I had a long discussion about what Adam asked me about if you three can watch the *Rock Follies* tonight. Even though my answer is "No, you can't," I think Gary and John, you two should say thank you to Adam now."

On the way up to school, Gary said, "I don't know why John and I had to bloody say thank you to you for asking Sir. It's not like we are able to watch the fucking programme."

I punched Gary hard in his back, which knocked him to the floor. "Fucking hell, Ad. What did you do that for? You wanker," Gary yelled out.

Then John shouted, "Stop, Ad, you fucking nutter."

"Piss off John or I'll start on you," I screamed back, kicking Gary about five times in his back as he lay on the corridor floor with blood dripping from his head, because he'd banged it on the wall as I pushed him over.

"Hey, hey, hey! What the hell is going on?" I heard a very angry voice shout behind me as I booted Gary one last time. "Adam King, pack that in right now," Mr. Eaton said, bounding up the corridor towards Gary as he said panicking, "John, go and get Sister Gray or Sister Peters quickly please, and if you pass a member of staff ask them to come here straight away? Adam, what just happened here?"

I began to get really scared as staff gathered around Gary, and before I was taken to Mr. Eaton's office, I heard Sister Gray saying "Can someone call 999 please? We need an ambulance."

'I'm really in the shit now,' I thought as John went off to class, and I was taken the other way to get the biggest telling off I will probably ever have in my bloody life. The sound of sirens in my ears were absolutely deafening, so much so that in Mr. Eaton's office I could just see mouths moving.

Very suddenly I heard the swish of curtains being drawn and then bright lights hitting my eyes. With that came voices which took me time to make out. Then I felt someone touch me on the arm and say, "Adam, good morning, it's time to get up for school."

"Gary, Gary. Where's Gary?" I screamed out, alarmingly, as Mr. Harwell said, "Adam, calm down and let me put you in your wheelchair. Then you can tell me what's wrong."

Mr. Jones, who was getting William dressed, called over, saying, "Is everything alright, Mr. Harwell?"

"I'm not sure. Adam is extremely anxious, and I am going to sit him in his chair to try and find out what the problem is," answered Mr. Harwell.

When I was up, I said, very worried and scared, "Please, Sir, let me talk to Gary and John?"

"Yes, Adam, I will, but you need to stop trembling. Just relax and take some deep breaths. That's a good boy."

As I took a few large deep breaths, Gary walked out of the bathroom, and I shouted, "Gary, come here please?"

"Yes, Adam. Are you okay, mate?" he said, making his way over towards Mr. Harwell and me.

"Your head? Your head? Can I have a look at the back please? Sorry, sorry I'm very sorry for hurting you and knocking you over," I replied almost in tears.

"Adam, I don't know what you're talking about. I'm fine, my head is good, it's still attached to my body. Adam, can I ask did you have a nightmare last night?" Gary asked, going back over to his bed to get dressed.

Then Mr. Harwell said, "Thank you, Gary, you've hit the nail right on the head."

Taking a big sigh, Sir carried on saying, as he stood up from sitting on my bed, "Right, Adam, let's go to the bathroom and give you a wash for school. After breakfast Mr. Jones and I would like to talk to you, Gary and John."

In my head I was screaming, 'Fuck no, please, that's where the whole bloody nightmare started from.' Perhaps it was a premonition.

Outside the medical room, John and I were waiting to be given our morning medication. John said, "Well Ad, you did your best, and we both knew Sir would say no, but thanks for asking him."

"That's alright, mate. I knew it was a long shot to ask if we could even stay up another hour."

"Open up, please, Adam. That's a good boy," Sister Gray said, putting my tablets in my mouth as she went on saying, "Are they gone? Would you like a drink of water?"

"No, thank you, Miss," I replied.

John then said, on our way to class, "I wonder what Mr. Read will have to say for himself today?"

"I don't know, John, but I'll tell you now, it better be something sensible because I am not working on the bloody sweet counter in Woollies!!"

"No, Ad, Stephen is likely to get that job!" John said, losing control of his wheelchair from laughing so much he crashed straight into the classroom door.

"Oh shit," he whispered, watching a lump of wood fall out of the classroom door frame. John looked over at me and mouthed, "HELP!!"

I just said, "What can I do? Oh and John, Mr. Eaton is walking down the corridor now, and I love you. So I'm going into class because I don't want to see you getting your arse kicked. Good luck mate!"

I went over to my Possum, and while we were waiting for our first lesson of the day, laughing at John trying to squirm his way out of having twenty-five lines, which were: *I must look where I am going when I am driving my electric wheelchair.*

Mrs. Farmstead walked past Mr. Eaton and John to come into class to take us for Maths. Mr. Eaton, following behind her, said, "Mrs. Farmstead, just to let you know the careers officer, Mr. Read, is in school today. So I would like to take the children to see him one at a time. After you have done registration could you send Adam to my office please?"

"Yes, not a problem, Mr. Eaton," replied Mrs. Farmstead.

I felt nervous about meeting Mr. Read, and he was going to ask me about what I might like to do after I leave school next year. Going along the corridor, my heart was pounding hard with nerves and excitement too. As I knew exactly what I wanted to do after leaving school. I had spoken to Mrs. Drew a lot about it over the past few years.

When I reached Mr. Eaton's office door, I just sat there for a few moments before I knocked. I said hello to Mrs. Pointer, Sir's secretary. She was a very lovely lady, kind, and if we needed any help or just to have a chat, Miss was always there for us.

On entering Mr. Eaton's office, I was met by Mr. Read. He was quite short, with black hair, and a curly black beard. He sat to the side of Mr. Eaton's desk and said, "Hello, Adam. It's good to meet you. Now today we are going to talk about what you might like to do after you leave school. Do you have any ideas yourself, Adam?"

I thought to myself, 'I suppose a train driver is out of the question!' as Mr. Eaton said, "Come on, Adam, answer the question please."

"I don't know, Sir. I'm really interested in drama. Mrs. Drew and I have spoken a lot about it in the past," I replied.

Mr. Read answered with a puzzled look, "Can I just ask, why drama, Adam?"

"I've always liked doing the classes, which I enjoyed and thought I was quite good at, Sir."

Mr. Read sat there fumbling through his notes when he suddenly said, "Unfortunately Adam, there's no drama colleges around that would be set up for your kind of needs or disability. However, we could have a look at some residential further education colleges and they will possibly have drama classes like you do in school. What do you think about that idea, Adam?"

"Are the colleges in London, Sir?" I said, because the thought of being away from home, I wasn't sure if I would like it. Even though going away to college might be totally different from school and if John comes with me, well that would be amazing!

Later that day John said, "Well, Ad, were you offered a job in the Bank of England by Mr. Read like Kenny, William and I were?"

"Why the fuck would Mr. Read even think any of you could do a job that sophisticated? Not unless they need you to be a runner at lunch times!"

"Adam, thank you so much for believing in us, you bastard."

"My dearest John, I don't live in a bloody fantasy world so I sodding well know we've all been offered to go to a residential further education college somewhere in Britain."

"Yeah, you're right, Ad, as bloody usual, but we have to make damn sure we go to the same college."

"Oh yes, that could be the making of us which would be fantastic."

Over the next few months or so, we all spent time visiting and having interviews at different colleges.

Especially Kenny, Gary, John and I, because we were all desperate to leave school. One morning I was going to my first class, which was English, when I passed Mrs. Drew in the corridor. Miss had always been one of my favourite teachers. I could talk to her about most things.

When she stopped me she said, "Good morning, Adam. How are you?"

"I'm fine, thank you, Miss, but I am in a bit of a hurry because I don't want to be late for class."

"No, Adam, of course you don't. I just wanted to ask how your interview went at Rosewater College. Did you like it?"

"Yes, Miss, it was all right, but I thought Wales was a bit too far."

"Okay, Adam, you better go to class now but can you come to see me at the end of the day, please?"

"Yes, Miss," I replied, going as fast as I could down the bloody corridor because I was five minutes late and Mr. Burns hated it if anyone wasn't in class on time, so I was right in the shit!!

"Why the fuck were you late for Burns class this morning? We left the boarding unit together," John whispered just as we were going on our first break.

"Well, well, well, who made you a bloody prefect in the ten minutes I wasn't in your presence!"

"Ad, I'm sorry mate. I just care."

"I was talking to Mrs. Drew about Rosewater College and she asked if she could see me after school today."

Then John raised his voice a bit, saying, "Lads, listen. Adam has got himself a hot date today after school!!"

"With a blind person, obviously," Gary said laughing.

"Can I say you are a lot of twats and for your information, it's with Mrs. Drew we are going to talk about colleges and other things, and if one of you says a word, I will have you stuffed!"

Kenny looked towards the back of his chair while he laughed, as Gary asked, "Would you like me to get your board out of your bag, Ken?" He gave a nod and a very large smile.

"Kenny, mate, I do like you, but if you say something derogatory to me, then I will do what I threatened!"

"God, Ad, I love it when you're masterful. Sorry Kenny, do carry on and just ignore the fat twit!"

Just before the bell rang for the end of our break, Gary said the words that Ken pointed to with his eyes and they were: *no one, looks, Adam, that way*!

"Kenny, you're a bloody shit!" I replied, giggling on the way to our next class.

CHAPTER 16

The summer of July 1979 was approaching speedily and Kenny, William and Gary had all accepted a place at Rosewater College. There was a part of me that was becoming sad because we were all very good friends. It was like a two-sided coin – we wanted to leave school desperately, but we knew how difficult it was going to be to leave each other. Even Stephen I would probably miss! I didn't quite know what Stephen was going to do after school as he kept everything to himself.

John and myself had been offered a place at a college in Manchester called St Andrews. It was a lovely place with large grounds and yes, they did drama, so I was very happy because I had two of the most important things in my life that meant the world to me: my John and drama.

"John," I said on a Friday, sitting in the playground a couple of weeks prior to leaving school. "God, it's bloody hot today."

"Yes it is, mate. I wish we could take off our ties and undo the top buttons of our shirts. At least from September we don't ever have to wear a fucking school uniform again in our lives."

"John, I'm going home tonight."

"I know, Ad, you told me that the other day. Is it time for you to go into an institution, and maybe not come to Manchester with me?"

"Firstly fuck off, and secondly, I am just excited about going home, as you know I don't go that often. I'm always stuck in this fucking place."

On Saturday morning after Dad had got me out of bed, and while he was feeding me my breakfast, the doorbell rang. It was April and Peter.

"Morning, love. How are you? More importantly, how's my beautiful grandson today?" Dad said, picking Peter out of his buggy.

"Your beautiful grandson is a bloody nightmare at the moment. He's teething so he screams all day and sodding night. I'm looking forward to having a break today and taking the other baby shopping," April said, about to give me the cup of coffee that was on the kitchen table as she went on to say, "Just shut your mouth and remember, there's a child in the room."

The coffee went everywhere because I was drinking and laughing. Then passing Peter to Mum for a cuddle, as she had just woken up, Dad shouted, "For heaven sakes, Adam. That was unnecessary. Now I'll have to put another t-shirt on you before you go shopping with April."

When I was being changed by Dad, I could hear Mum and April talking in the kitchen and Mum said, "April, Adam has £100 to buy clothes to go to his new college. Can you please go to shops like Marks & Spencer or British Home Stores? However, if your dad and I had our way, he would be staying on at school until he was ruddy eighteen, to get him away from that damn boy. He is the one that is putting all of these disgusting thoughts into your brother's head."

As I sat in my bedroom ready to go out, I felt so fucked off and angry because if I'd brought home a girl like Sean does sometimes, it would all be just fine and bloody dandy. April came into my room and asked, "Would you like to hold your nephew before we go?"

"But of course. He's the only sane one in this pissing family," I replied, as April supported me to cuddle him.

Dad dropped us off in the high street. I said to April just outside Woolworths - but before I could get a blooming word out of my mouth April interrupted me, raising her voice and saying, "No, Adam, we aren't going into Woolworths today. We are here to buy your new clothes for when you go to Nottingham."

I was really annoyed as I absolutely screamed at her in the middle of the high street, "That wasn't what I was going to fucking say, you stupid bitch! I heard you and Mum talking earlier about me and I wanted to ask if we could go for a coffee so I could have a chat with you, as I thought you understood, but I was bloody wrong."

"Ad, I'm very sorry to have assumed what you were going to say. Yes, let's go for a coffee now. Come on, darling, stop crying. People are looking at you."

"I couldn't give a fuck."

When I had calmed down, April and I went into a Lyons cafe to have an iced bun and a coffee. We sat at a table and as usual I felt very self-conscious from all the staring. However, as April took a bite of her bun, I said, "April, do you understand I'm gay, and it wasn't John that put things in my head like Mum said this morning? If you must know, I was the first one to make a move on him when I was eleven at a school swimming gala."

Putting a towel around my neck and giving me the first bite of my bun, she replied, "I'm fine with you being gay, but I'm a bit shocked that you knew from such an early age. Why didn't you tell me then? Now Adam, you know Mum and Dad are never ever going to be able to accept this, don't you? Also one last question, Ad. Are you going to Nottingham just to be with John?"

Sitting back down opposite me, I began to feel a bit cross as I said, "Yes, you're right. It is about him, but it's also that they offer drama too, and that has been my love for a long time. So one day I hope to be an actor."

On leaving the cafe to carry on shopping April gave a laugh and said, "Not that old chestnut again. I thought Mum had spoken to you about how impossible that would be for you."

"Fuck off! Nobody has faith in me," I shouted back as we went into Marks & Spencer.

I didn't understand why we had to go to this bloody shop. It's so bloody expensive, and if we didn't spend the whole sodding one hundred pounds on clothes, I could buy a couple of albums.

"Right, Ad, we have most of your clothes except for socks and pants. Let's go to the underwear department."

"April," I said quite sheepishly, as I felt embarrassed knowing what was about to come out of my mouth. "Can I buy some white briefs, please?"

"No Adam. You know Mum told me to get y-fronts for you. Anyway what the bloody hell do you want briefs for?"

"The truth is John said he likes to see boys just in them. Especially..."

"Don't continue with that sentence please, and I can't believe you want to buy sexy underwear out of Mum's and Dad's money!"

"For God's sake, I'm sixteen. I should be entitled to buy my own fucking pants!"

April pushed me over to the cashier whilst giggling and calling me a silly bugger. When we had paid for my clothes, which came to £87, April said, "We have just enough money to buy one pack of three briefs, but on your head be it when Mum asked you why you wanted them. I so would love to watch you squirm out of that one."

When April was pushing me home from the high street over all the fucking lumps and bumps in the pavement, I was sitting there contemplating everything as April said, about half way from home, "What's wrong with you? You're very quiet and that's unusual for you."

"Do shut up, you silly cow. I'm thinking about my life and what's to come," I replied.

Turning into the street where we lived, April said in an excited voice, "Look Ad, there's Dad holding Peter in the front garden."

Mum in the lounge, taking the bags off the back of my wheelchair, said, "I see you bought your clothes in Marks & Spencer. Let me have a look to make sure I approve. April, how much did your brother spend?"

Jumping in before April opened her trap and without bloody thinking, I blurted out, "£88 Mum."

"Are you sure, Adam?"

"Yes, Mum, of course I am."

Just as I said that I thought, 'Fuck the briefs!'

"Right, Adam, if it cost £88, then why has April given me only £5 change when it should be £12 that I should have in my hand?"

The room fell silent just as Dad entered with Peter, who put his arms out to go to April. Dad whispered, smirking as he sat down next to Mum, "What's wrong, love, has someone died?"

"Mum, Dad, I need to take Peter home. He's getting restless."

"All right, my love. Thanks for taking Adam out. Let me give my grandson a kiss goodbye."

As April brought Peter over to give Mum and Dad a cuddle, I thought, 'Fucking hell, talk about a rat leaving a sinking ship.'

Monday of the very last week had arrived and everybody was giddy with excitement.

Gary said, bobbing his head around like he was on drugs, "I bloody love the last week of the summer term. We hardly do any work, and especially this week as we don't ever have to come to this crap place again after Friday. HURRAH, HURRAH fucking HURRAH!"

PETE EDWARDS (1963-2022)

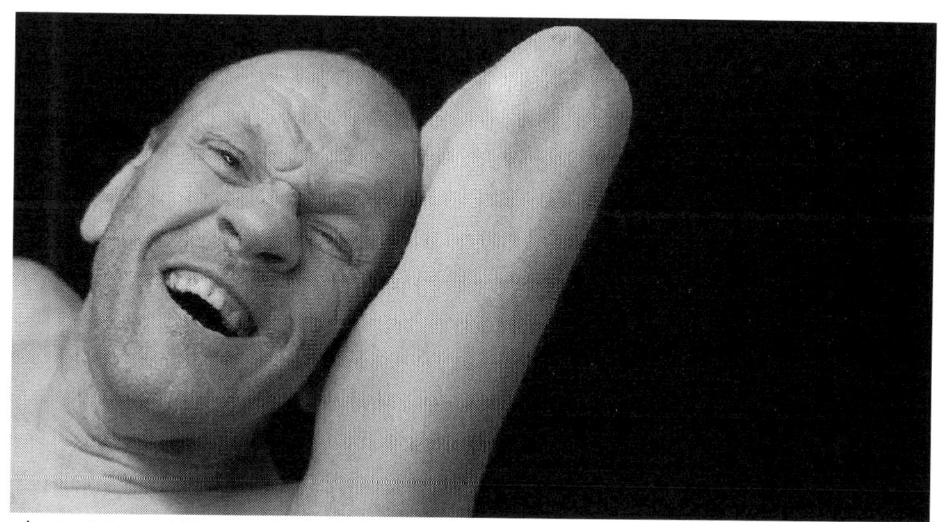

photo: Manuel Vason

Pete Edwards was an actor, writer, director and workshop leader. As a queer, disabled artist with a differing speech pattern, Pete pioneered new forms of writing and performance and blazed a trail for other artists.

In 2004-05, Pete attended and graduated from Graeae Theatre's Missing Piece - an actor's training course for disabled performers – where he devised a monologue that was subsequently expanded into a full evening of performance, *FAT*. Melding striking language, inventive movement and visual imagery, *FAT* chronicles one man's search for love as he travels across London's South Bank. *FAT* premiered at Oval House Theatre in 2009 before touring across the UK, including at DaDa Fest in Liverpool where Pete won the award for Best Emerging Performer (2010). He subsequently took the show to the Edinburgh fringe in 2012, supported by the Arts Council's East of England programme.

Additional acting work included roles in a short film, *Welcome Stop*, written and directed by Michael Achtman, and *Purposeless Movements* with Scotland's Birds of Paradise Theatre Company. Pete was an Associate Artist with filmpro, a London-based digital arts organisation, and devised a performance workshop for people with differing speech at the Barbican Centre and Guildhall School of Theatre and Music.

In 2014, he was awarded an Unlimited R&D commission for a project exploring themes of rape and sexual abuse of disabled people. He delivered accessible drama workshops for RAWD in Liverpool, and presented at the IntegrART conference in Geneva and at the Live Art Development Agency's Access All Areas conference in London.

Pete was getting his first novel, *Why Isn't School More Like Shopping*, ready for publication when he passed away unexpectedly in 2022.

filmpro would like to thank Nick Williams for his assistance in preparing this manuscript for publication. Publishing team: Michael Achtman, Çağlar Kimyoncu, Zeynep Dağlı

filmpro is a digital arts organisation striving for a creative world that champions diversity, inclusivity and innovation.

www.filmpro.org/pete-edwards